HAVING HER ENEMY'S SECRET SHIFTER BABY

A HOWLS ROMANCE

CELIA KYLE
MARINA MADDIX

CLASSIC ROMANCE WITH A FURRY TWIST

BLURB

*S*he's pregnant and he's determined to have her under his roof and in his bed...no matter the cost!

Reese can't get the delectable she-wolf Jane Coleman out of his mind. They shared one passionate night on a Ft. Lauderdale beach and she disappeared by morning. He should forget her, but his wolf won't let him dismiss the memories of her silken skin, lush curves, and seductive smile.

Even as he fights to keep his lands out of the hands of a rival pack, he can't suppress his constant craving for the female werewolf. The last place he expects to find the alluring stranger is at the side of his sworn enemy—her father.

He should crush her father and walk away, but one sniff changes Reese's plans. Jane is pregnant with his pup and he will have them both!

CHAPTER 1

"*S*hots, Jane. *Shots!*" Elizabeth slurred and wrapped her thin arm around Jane's shoulders.

Jane Coleman smiled at her friend and unwound herself from Elizabeth's grasp. Elizabeth's breath could knock a fire-breathing dragon out of the night sky. "Don't you think you've had plenty? Come on. I want to dance."

"It's not me I'm worried about," Elizabeth complained, slouching to one side as she spoke, almost like a marionette without a puppeteer. "You've barely had anything to drink all night."

That, strictly speaking, was true. She'd had two beers on the beach earlier in the day and one Cosmo

CELIA KYLE & MARINA MADDIX

since they'd arrived at the bar, but she knew better than to get tipsy around her human friends. Tipsy werewolves were dangerous werewolves. Lowered inhibitions tempted her to shift into her wolf form. And as much as she loved the idea of sprinting down the beach, the sea breeze fluttering through her strawberry-blonde fur... the sight of a wolf running around a Ft. Lauderdale beach at the height of spring break might cause a panic. A tiny one.

Plus, after one too many, it was too easy to forget she had to treat humans like porcelain or she might accidentally hurt someone. Normal human girls— like she was pretending to be—weren't able to pick up a coffee table and chuck it across the room with one hand. Hell, her freshman year, she nearly tore a frat boy's arm clean off when he grabbed her ass at a party. She'd experienced a twinge of regret that he'd lost his baseball scholarship because she dislocated his shoulder, but he certainly learned never to grope a woman without her permission.

"You know I don't drink much," Jane reminded her friend. "I just want to dance." She tugged on Elizabeth's arm. "Come dance with me!"

Elizabeth slouched away like a ragdoll and bumped gracelessly against the bar. "Please? One shot. We'll toast to graduation."

"That's months away."

"Oh, please! Everyone knows you're going to graduate top of the class." Elizabeth rolled her eyes. "We should celebrate!"

Though Elizabeth's "celebrate" sounded more like *celibate* and Jane's wolf pawed at her. It was not a big fan of the word "celibate" and liked to remind her of that. Often.

"You're right, it's *you* we have to worry about," Jane teased. "Fine, one shot, but no more after this. One and *done*."

"Fine." Elizabeth sounded like her tongue was a little too big for her mouth. "What're we drinking?"

Jane smiled broadly at the bartender, which was all it took to grab his attention. He practically stopped mid-pour and rushed to them.

"What can I get you, ladies?"

"Two shots of Don Julio with lime and salt, please." Jane beamed and he blinked.

"Sure thing."

He dashed back to the other side of the bar, and Elizabeth snorted and rolled her eyes.

"What?" Jane frowned at her friend.

"You."

"What'd *I* do?"

"I think it's magic. You have some weird voodoo, dick whisperer, pied piper of the penis thing. It's like a supernatural power. You just have to think you want a guy's attention and then—" Elizabeth snapped her fingers. Or tried. She couldn't get her fingertips to touch each other and stared at her hand cross-eyed for a while before finally giving up and flailing her hands instead. "*Poof!* He's there."

Jane snorted as if Elizabeth's words were ridiculous. She couldn't let on that her friend was way too close to the truth. "I'm just like everyone else."

"Nope, uh uh, no way," Elizabeth said, as the bartender set their drinks in front of them.

"Thanks," Jane said with a flirty smile, tossing her long, strawberry blonde hair over her shoulder.

"No problem. This round's on me." He winked at Jane and then moved down the bar to help some other hapless maiden. It wasn't until he was out of sight that she noticed he'd written his number on her cocktail napkin.

"Smooth," Elizabeth sniffed. "How do I get them to do that? Or is it all about the boobage?" Elizabeth stared down at her own cleavage and jiggled her tits. "Do your job, dammit."

Jane laughed. "What are you talking about? You've got *great* boobs."

Elizabeth sighed, tossed back her shot, and then slammed the empty glass on the bar. She hissed as the tequila burned its way down her throat. "Don't pretend you're not built like one of those sexy mud flap girls."

Jane quirked a brow and slid the shot glass out of her friend's reach. "I think you've had plenty to drink now."

Elizabeth always got like this when she drank. As a lifelong dancer, her frame was lean and wispy. She had very little in the chesticle region and next to no junk in her trunk.

And her point of comparison?

Jane. Always Jane. Or mud flaps, but that always circled back to Jane anyway.

It was one of the human quirks Jane had never understood and her wolf woofed its agreement. In the pack, no one focused on appearance. Okay, maybe it was only Jane who didn't care. She'd never dressed to flaunt her bountiful curves. As the daughter of the alpha, it wouldn't be seemly—or so he insisted.

"Elizabeth, let's dance. I'm sick of standing around."

Elizabeth shook her head and wobbled precariously. "No way. I'm heading back up to the room. If I try to dance, I'll fall over."

Jane felt a whisper of disappointment at calling it a night so early, but her bestie needed her. "Okay, let's go."

Elizabeth shook her head. "No, you stay and have fun. Enjoy yourself. I'll see you in the morning."

Jane tracked Elizabeth as she made her way into the hotel and kept an eye on her through the floor-to-ceiling windows until she boarded an elevator. Then she turned her attention to the darkened beach. The bar sat on the edge of the sand, lights casting a soft glow across the beach.

A handful of lovebirds danced at the edge of the circle of light, kicking up the sugary powder as they moved and dancing slowly despite the rapid beat of the music. She was tempted to move to the black space just beyond them, where she could see the stars glittering on the ocean's surface like fireflies. Where she could be swallowed in the dark and enjoy being a faceless presence. She could do whatever she wanted and there wouldn't be anyone to tell her it was "unseemly."

Jane shook her head and made her way to the middle of the dance floor. She'd agreed to hit the bar with Elizabeth because she'd been promised dancing. Dammit, she was going to dance.

Shafts of light flashed in the delighted faces of the people crammed on the dance floor. The DJ's light show was synced with the music, flashing a different color with every beat while the crowd jumped and danced to the up-tempo song. Just as quickly as the energy rose, it gradually settled into a gentle sway when a slower song filled the air. Jane closed her eyes and lost herself in the music, feeling the notes flow through her while she found her rhythm.

This was her time, her chance to unwind before the end of her career as a college student. After that? Her life would begin. Her *human* life. She'd find a job in her field of study—*art history 4 lyfe*—and do her best to "fit in." Shifting wouldn't be a part of her life anymore. Her wolf whined like it always did and Jane fought against giving in to that pitiful cry. It knew she'd become immune to its pouting and switched to growls instead, snarling its objection. It didn't want to be turned into a second-class citizen inside her two-legged body.

She'd been born a werewolf. Why couldn't she just be happy being a werewolf?

Jane mentally sighed. She had plans. Eventually she'd find a nice human man with his nice, boring human life, and then they'd settle down with a house and a white picket fence.

Couldn't it see the benefit to a life in the suburbs? No fighting. No dominance games. No alpha telling her how to live her life or declare her actions "unseemly"?

She seriously hated that word.

Jane got back to reminding her wolf of "the plan."

Children were out of the question, of course. She'd heard that mixed-breed babies had more trouble controlling their shifts than full-blooded wolves. She wouldn't be able to hide her true nature if she had to control a feral child and she was determined not to risk being discovered.

Of course, her parents wouldn't like her decision, especially her domineering father.

Her wolf nudged her, telling her that it agreed with her dad and she shouldn't turn her back on her wolf heritage. She pushed the beast to the back of her mind, shoving it away from her surface thoughts. It retreated with an echoing growl, telling her that she should be thankful to have such a good alpha.

And her father really was a good alpha to the Coleman pack, but she couldn't wait to be out from under his thumb and away from Wilde Mountain. He expected so much from her... Too much. She'd never asked to be the daughter of an alpha, so why should she have to abide by his arbitrary rules?

Rejecting life in the pack would be unthinkable, as far as he was concerned, and she had no doubt he'd put up a fight.

A wave of sadness washed over her and she closed her eyes. Lights flashed orange behind her closed eyelids and she struggled to move with the blood-thumping beat of the music.

As much as she hated the idea of staying with the pack, she'd also miss her parents—her mother's smiling face and father's grumbles and growls. But she had no choice. She *would* live life on her own terms, and if her father couldn't accept that, she'd go somewhere her pack could never find her.

A hacker at school had already agreed to create her new identity... for a price. All that was left was to pick a place her family would never think to look for her and her life could begin.

And she only had a few months left.

Excitement overrode the twinge of sadness. Biting back a smile, Jane lost herself in the music again, rolling her hips along with the bassline and dropping low every now and then. Without anyone around her she felt freer than she had in years. She let her hair swish across her back as she moved.

But like all good things, it had to come to an end.

Something—*someone*—bumped against her back, and weak human hands slid around her waist. The stink of sweat, cloying cologne, and alcohol stung her nose and she tried to shimmy away, hoping the guy would get the hint and let her go.

He didn't.

Instead, he gripped her tighter, pulled her ass into his crotch and whispered in her ear. "I like the way you move, baby."

Baby? She wasn't his baby.

Her inner wolf wanted to turn around and teach the human male why it was a bad idea to lay his hands on a werewolf. With one hand, she'd grip his wrist so hard his bones splintered. With the other... she'd ensure baby-making wasn't in his future. Ever.

This stranger wasn't an alpha, hence, not worthy of

her. Except... Accepting the touch of human males was part of assimilating into human life, right? No human male could compare to the strength of even the weakest wolf, much less the alpha her position in the pack demanded.

She groaned and her wolf snarled. She'd have to get used to being around weak men. It was a sacrifice she was willing to make if it meant living life on her own terms.

But that didn't mean they were allowed to rub their unimpressive members against her ass. Shaking her head, Jane gently pulled away. She wasn't going to make a scene by breaking the dude's arm. Unfortunately, the guy was an idiot. A drunk idiot, but still an idiot. He caught her wrist and tugged her back against him once more.

"Don't leave, angel. You're perfect right where you are."

"Not so much," she yelled above the music.

"We're just getting started."

"No, you're not."

The voice was deep and gruff and unfamiliar, and it set the hairs on her arms standing on end. So much more masculine than the whining tenor of the man who'd been grinding up on her. The warm evening air whispered over the crowd, delicate flavors of the sea intermingled with the aroma of those around her. Then she caught his scent.

Not bland or vague like human men. He was all musk, mountain air, and leather. Scents that crept into her and taunted her wolf. Exactly the way a man ought to smell.

Jane craned her neck to get a good look at him, but only a dark shadow slanted out from a commandingly tall frame. In the span of a blink, the human was ripped away and this new man took his place. Strong hands grasped her hips and a muscular body aligned with her curves. She melted into his firm touch, moving with the music without thinking as she breathed him in. His scent teased and taunted her, making her head spin with the flavors.

God, nobody had smelled this tempting in years. Not since she'd left her pack. Not since...

She breathed deeper and caught a rustic woodiness that was all too familiar. If she didn't know any better, she'd guess he was a wolf too. But that was impossible, right?

Of all the random bars in all the random states, what

were the odds two wolves would wind up dancing together in the same beachside bar?

Jane's brain wanted her to turn and ask him, but her body wanted to continue moving in perfect time with his. So, she remained silent and let her body take the lead, reveling in the hard lines of his abs and a particularly tempting hardness against her ass. The more they danced, the more Jane was sure the man overwhelming her with his mere scent wasn't human.

He gripped her hips tighter as a new song began, and her wolf purred with happiness. With him snug against her, Jane ached for him to explore her body, to turn her around and let her feel every massive inch of his body hidden beneath his tight jeans.

Yet his hands stayed in place as her heartbeat soared.

Seriously? This was insane. She didn't even know what the dude looked like, but already her body howled for him to take her. She wanted him to run his work-calloused palms over her breasts and tease her right there on the dance floor. She felt more alive than ever—swaying with the music and allowing her body to move as she desired.

She rolled her hips, rubbing her ass against this

man's growing need. Heat raced through her, a desperate throb taking up residence at the juncture of her thighs. She repeated the tempting move and figured it'd only be minutes before he finally lost control and took her. All she had to do was get him there.

The song switched again and a deep, rumbling bassline echoed the low pulse of need between her thighs. Swiveling her hips in time with the music, Jane pushed her ass up against him a hint harder, delighting in his surprised gasp.

"You're trying to tease me," he growled in her ear. That deep rumble had the tips of her breasts tightening into hard pebbles.

"Is it working?" she whispered in return.

Gripping her harder, he spun her to face him and held her just as snugly as he before. She faced a broad wall of muscle covered by a loose linen shirt tucked neatly into a pair of snug jeans. It took every ounce of strength for Jane not to sink her fangs into his flesh and claim him. Hopefully he wouldn't see how badly she drooled at the idea.

It felt like it took a year for her to crane her neck far enough to meet the stranger's gaze. Then her heartbeat stuttered.

For a moment, all she could see were harsh lines, and then his feral beauty came into focus. His jaw was made of stone, and his light brown eyes held mesmerizing flecks of gold. She couldn't tear her gaze away, even if she wanted to.

Without a word, his eyes flickered from brown to a glowing amber, confirming her suspicions. Whatever the odds, he was a werewolf, and somehow they'd found each other. When she flashed her own amber eyes, he growled in approval.

"Thought so," he muttered, his eyes never wavering from hers—more amber than brown now. "Name?"

"Jane. You?"

"Reese."

The rumble of his animalistic voice sent another thrill of pleasure straight to her core. She could probably come right there if he'd just keep talking.

His next words took her right to the edge. "Let's go."

It wasn't a question and she didn't mind his demanding tone one bit.

Thick, warm fingers wrapped around her hand and Jane followed along eagerly as he led her through the crowd. His restraint at not tearing everyone in their way to shreds was admirable and everything, but Jane's wolf howled at her to get down to business already. She had a scratch that only Reese could reach. She wanted him more than anything or anyone else in her entire life.

Being so close to him, covered in his scent and body prepared to accept every inch of his cock...

Nothing had ever felt more right.

CHAPTER 2

*R*eese gripped Jane's hand and guided her through the crowd, his wolf howling in approval. He'd found a female—a strong, delicious wolf female—and he couldn't wait to get her to his den.

Er, his hotel room.

He reached the wide breezeway that led to the hotel doors, only to feel a strong hand grab his shoulder. Brody, his beta and best friend, stepped in front of Reese, his arms crossed over his barrel of a chest. Reese's wolf snarled its objection at being delayed. The beast wanted to cover Jane in their scent. Now.

"Whatever it is, it can wait," Reese growled. He

pulled Jane in tightly behind him and hoped Brody would get the hint.

Brody's gaze drifted over the girl—which set Reese's teeth on edge—and then focused on his friend again. "No, it can't."

When Reese didn't budge, Brody leaned in and whispered, "You don't want to do this."

Again, Brody's eyes flicked over to Jane. No matter their history, if Brody looked at Jane again...

"I assure you, *I do*," Reese growled, staring his friend down, but Brody only moved to stand more squarely in Reese's path.

"Reese, listen—" Brody started, but Reese snarled and let a little of his wolf out. His eyes burned as brown bled to full amber and his gums ached as his fangs descended.

"If you want to keep your hide intact, you'll step aside."

The two men stared each other down for a long moment, and Reese wondered if he'd have to pin his beta to the concrete. They remained in place, neither of them flinching, until Brody finally let his gaze lower to the ground.

His beta stepped aside, but just as Reese pushed past

him, Brody spoke one last time. "You better remember I tried to stop you."

Reese ignored him. The only thing that mattered was getting Jane to his room. Then they could ravage each other like the animals they were. Once inside the posh hotel, he jabbed the elevator button repeatedly, willing it to hurry.

Whatever ate at Brody could wait until morning—along with everything else. Tonight, he wasn't the alpha of the Warren pack. He wasn't in Ft. Lauderdale on pack business, searching for a way to end the conflict between his pack and another. His sole purpose was to make Jane scream with a kind of pleasure she'd never experienced.

A pleasure he ached for, himself. Pressure had been building since his father died, leaving him to lead his pack. He'd tried to find solace in the arms of the women in his pack, but none had provided the distraction he desperately needed. But this beautiful stranger would take his mind off his newfound responsibilities.

Between her long, strawberry blonde waves and curves in all the right places... she was a gorgeous, tempting distraction. Every time he looked at her, he found something new to lust after. He couldn't wait to peel away her skin-tight red tank top and see exactly what lay underneath.

Knowing she was a wolf just like him, he didn't bother to limit his strength. He pulled her into the elevator car, thankful no one else occupied the space. One arm wrapped around Jane, he quickly slid his keycard into the control panel. Now they'd have a nonstop trip to his penthouse suite. The moment the doors slipped shut once again, he pulled her to him and buried his face in her neck. A deep breath brought him more of her tantalizing scent and he couldn't withhold the groan that filled his chest.

"My God, you're gorgeous," he murmured, his voice ragged to his own ears. "Smell s'good."

His cock throbbed in his slacks, length straining his pants.

Jane moaned in response, the sound like a physical touch. One that wrapped around his dick and stroked him from base to tip. That was all the permission he needed to take what they *both* desired.

Reese slipped his fingers into her hair and fisted the silken strands. He used his grip to tip her head back and urge her onto her toes. Now their lips were mere millimeters apart. The heat from her panting breaths nearly destroyed him, urging him to capture her mouth with his own, but he couldn't stop staring into her pale green eyes. His breath caught in his throat and he was utterly hypnotized by her beauty. When she whined and squirmed against him, he knew it was time to act and he lowered his head toward hers.

The moment their lips touched, he lost whatever sense remained. All that mattered was Jane—touching and kissing every part of her.

No woman had ever felt this perfect in his embrace and his inner wolf howled its agreement. It urged him to take, to claim. Take her body until she was coated in his scent.

She yielded to him, sinking into his kiss with passionate abandon. But that didn't mean she was a passive partner. She clung to him, fingers fisting his shirt and pulling him tighter against her. Her tongue swept out to meet his, deepening their kiss and taunting him at the same time. She met him stroke for stroke, her passion rising to meet his until they fed off each other's need.

The scent of her desire filled the small space, her slick pussy ready for his cock.

Fuck. Eternity wouldn't be long enough for Reese to get his fill of Jane's lush body. His hands freely roamed her curves, cupping the roundness of her ass and exploring the swell of her breasts. The warmth from her aroused flesh burned him and he ached to touch her without the barrier of clothing.

Jane broke their kiss with a rough gasp, her chest heaving with her panting breaths. "Do you think there are cameras in here?"

A shudder of desire slithered down his spine. "Who cares?"

Her body trembled and she pulled away, giving him a wicked grin—wicked and hungry. Then she licked her plump lips and dropped to her knees.

"Oh, fuck," he grunted as she made quick work of his zipper.

For a brief flash, he wondered if he should stop her and insist on waiting until they reached his room. But any ability to think vanished the second her fingers wrapped around his stiff cock and pulled him free of his jeans.

He'd never seen a more beautiful sight, a gorgeous woman on her knees, lips parted to take his cock deep... His length twitched and she caressed the tip of his shaft with her thumb, rubbing away the drop of pre-cum decorating the mushroomed head.

"Fuck, Jane," he rasped and watched as she brought her mouth closer to his hardness. Any moment now she'd take him into her mouth and...

In his final lucid moment, he slammed his palm against the emergency stop button. The alarm released a piercing ring, but neither paid any attention.

Not when Jane's eyes sparkled with dark hunger. Eyes on him and with a teasing smile, she stroked him so slowly he thought he might lose his damned mind. She added a small twist, her movements increasing in pace as she gripped him tighter. She pumped him over and over again, holding off on giving him what they both craved. As if she read his mind, she grinned and flicked her tongue past her plump lips.

"Suck it," his command came out as barely more than a growl.

Jane whimpered as if she'd been eagerly awaiting his order and then dipped her head until he could no longer see her eyes. She moved slowly, flicking her tongue here and there, the barely-there caresses driving him to the brink of insanity. Reese gripped the handrail until his knuckles ached. If he didn't restrain himself, he'd bury his fingers in her hair and force his dick down her throat. For her to take all of him and give him so much pleasure... Fuck. He had no doubt that would happen at some time during the night.

Gazing down as she explored him, he wished he could capture the image forever. This woman on her knees, accepting all he had to offer. Just as he committed the details to memory, her lips took him in fully and his world flipped upside down. Breath whooshed from his lungs and he was barely aware of his movements. He wove his fingers into her hair while she gingerly obeyed his previous command.

Suck it.

Her mouth was warm and welcoming, and he allowed his head to fall back against the wall. She took him in inch by inch, until the head of his cock nudged the back of her throat.

"Fuck. Yes, just like that," he hissed. His dick throbbed and twitched inside her wet heat. His balls ached for release, to flood her mouth with his cum.

Jane hummed her agreement and the vibrations ricocheted across his nerve endings. The vibrations sent him spiraling toward the edge of bliss. A tingle ran up his spine, and his balls tightened as she slid her head back and then down again.

Damn but he was close. So fucking close.

What he wouldn't give to let go of all control and allow her to take him past the brink. Watching her swallow everything he had to give would be a dream come true, but the promise of more stopped him. He recalled the way her body moved against his on the dance floor, how she ground her ass into him. How her body begged him to take her. No, the night wouldn't end until he knew every inch of this woman and they were both too exhausted to move.

Reese mustered the will to stop and let his head drop forward. Fuck, that was a mistake. Staring down at her, seeing her legs spread wide enough that her very tiny, very tight skirt had rolled up to her waist. A lacy red thong peeked out from underneath, teasing him as her body moved. He gripped the bar behind him even tighter and struggled against the urge to take her on the floor of the elevator. He had no idea who this woman was, but he was powerless against her.

Especially when her lips were wrapped around his cock.

Groaning with effort, Reese uncurled the fingers of

one hand from the railing and gently pushed her away. She slowly dragged her mouth along his shaft and caught his eye when she carefully released his cock. She smiled as she wiped the corner of her mouth and then slowly stood.

Jane didn't seem to give a damn that her skirt remained caught around her waist. She turned and bent to push the emergency button, ending that annoying alarm.

It would have only taken a flick to move the thin scrap of fabric aside and make her his. Then the elevator jerked alive and he managed to stuff himself back into his jeans, cursing the rough fabric as it scraped his sensitive flesh.

Still, he couldn't let a perfectly good ass go to waste. He gripped her hips and pulled her back. He pressed against her for the rest of the ride, reveling in the way she moved her hips in slow, rhythmic circles. He slipped his hand down the front of the skimpy thong, and Jane gasped and arched against him in response. Evidence of her need coated his fingers, her slick wetness teasing him with her tempting warmth.

An ache he'd never experienced consumed him. He'd never desired a woman so fully in his life. So completely.

The elevator dinged and doors slid open to reveal the penthouse suite. He didn't hesitate to sweep Jane into his arms and carry her into his temporary home.

Reese let himself go, releasing a growl of need as he carried her through the ridiculously luxurious suite. He couldn't move fast enough, his shoes beating a staccato on the polished marble floor.

She wasn't idle as he moved down the hall, her teasing lips and talented tongue kissing and licking his neck. His wolf howled its approval, overjoyed when her teeth scraped his skin and the desperate need for her bite assaulted him. His own fangs lengthened in response, piercing his gums and emerging in preparation.

First fuck, then claim. The words pounded through his veins, the drive increasing with every step.

Fuck. Claim. Fuck. Claim.

Reese turned one last corner and reached the bedroom, striding into the room without hesitation. He tossed Jane onto the massive bed and she bounced on the cushioned surface. She lay there, sprawled and panting heavily, waiting for him. Those bright red panties lured him, calling him forward and he crept closer.

With a flick of his wrist and slice of his wolf's claws, her top lay in tatters, revealing a sheer red bra underneath—tiny scraps of silk and lace that matched those wicked panties. His mouth watered at the sight of her hard nipples straining against the delicate fabric.

Crawling over her like a hunter claiming his prey, he lowered his head and sucked one into his mouth. Jane cried out and arched against him, giving him access to the clasp in the back. He reached behind her and tugged on the clasp, claw parting the cloth with ease. He caught the cup of her bra with his teeth and tugged, pulling the lace away from his prize. Those dusky pink nubs beckoned him, begging to be sucked and flicked. Would her skin taste as sweet and sinful as her mouth?

Probably better.

And he couldn't wait to test that theory, but not before he got his cock inside her. Hard. Deep.

And all fucking night long.

He retreated and pulled her bra from her body, tossing the lacy garment over his shoulder. Then he eased back and withdrew from the bed, reaching for the thin sides of her panties. He hooked his fingers beneath the elastic and tugged, drawing that small barrier down her legs. The moment he tossed the bit of silk away, Jane parted her legs, revealing his prize. Dark blonde curls hid her pussy from his view, dampness clinging to the closely cropped strands. Her pink flesh teased him, urging him to come closer for a taste.

Soon.

Reese reached for the buttons of his shirt, quickly releasing each one until it slipped from his shoulders and fell to the ground. Next, he toed off his shoes and worked on his pants. Wolf's claws made handling the button and zipper difficult, but he was motivated. He wasn't going to let a little thing like clothing get in the way of having Jane.

Jane's hands went to her skirt, tugging at the lower hem, and he grasped her wrist before she could move another inch.

"No," he growled. "That stays on. Stockings and heels, too."

The black thigh highs and four inch heels had been driving him crazy. Pushing the skirt back up to her waist, he stood back for a long moment to admire the gorgeous creature in front of him. Her body was everything it had promised to be—plump curves and pale skin. The swell of her breasts and ass were enough to make him want to spend a month exploring every inch of her body.

He wanted to lock them both in the hotel room and stay there for eternity, discovering new ways to make each other cry out with pleasure.

But they only had one night.

Reese grasped her ankles and tugged her closer until her ass rested on the very edge of the mattress. "Turn over, feet on the ground, that pretty ass on display for me."

And in the perfect position for him to slide right into that hot pussy.

Jane obeyed, twisting her body and arching her back to put the curve of her ass on full display.

Damn if this girl didn't know exactly what she was doing.

JANE HAD NO IDEA WHAT SHE WAS DOING, BUT SHE *DID* know she didn't want to stop. One look from him and her pussy clenched. One gentle touch and her clit twitched. As for the feel of his cock in her mouth...

She'd never done that before—had never wanted to do such a thing—but it'd felt right with Reese. Right and wicked at the same time.

She moved into position without hesitation, feet on the ground and pussy on display. Cold air bathed her heated flesh, sending a new tendril of longing through her. She'd never been so alive with desire in her life, never craved another so badly she was willing to do *anything* to feel him inside her. Blood thundered in her ears and drowned her ability to hear. But she didn't need to hear in order to feel Reese's every touch.

Her wolf whimpered and whined, her animal anxious to be claimed. It longed to feel Reese's wolf break the flesh of her neck, to claim her as his mate. His scent drugged her, lulled her wolf's inhibitions until the animal could think of nothing but being taken by the large alpha.

Which was impossible.

Not only was she trying to establish life outside of a pack, but she had no idea where—and which pack —Reese called home. All she knew was that he was tall and chiseled, muscles practically cut from stone, and his scent tempted her to throw caution to the wind. With every breath, she had to fight her wolf that much harder. The beast was determined to receive Reese's bite.

Jane glanced over her shoulder, hair tickling her back as she whipped her head to the side. She wanted to gauge Reese's reaction, see what *he* thought of her body. One look was all she needed to see that the big bad wolf liked what he had spread bare in front of him. His eyes were pure amber and sprinklings of fur dotted his cheeks then flowed down his neck. He was bare from waist up, those muscles on display. As for waist *down*... His pants still clung to his hips, balancing on the deeply carved muscles.

It'd only take one nudge for them to pool at his feet. One nudge to reveal all of him—including that thick, glorious cock. Her mouth watered, memories of his dick in her mouth making her ache for more.

"So beautiful," he murmured and reached for her. He traced the curve of her spine, single finger skating over her sensitive skin. He didn't stop when he reached the top of her ass. No, he continued, teasing the wicked pucker between her ass cheeks and on until he reached her pussy. He ran that fingertip up and down her slit, giving her pleasure yet still holding it just out of reach.

"So wet for me, aren't you?" His voice turned rough

with the growl of his wolf. He dipped between her lower lips, sliding easily through her cream until he found her clit.

A lightning bolt of pleasure speared her, entire body thrumming with need at that caress. Jane moaned and then whimpered, wiggling her ass as she sought more of his touch. And he gave it to her. He circled and tapped her clit, taunting that bundle of nerves with a tempo that had her clawing at the bed. Her nails emerged, sharp tips digging into the blanket and slicing the fabric with ease. She should care about the damage, but...

But that was when Reese slid his other hand up her spine, stopping when he reached the base of her neck. He gave her a gentle squeeze and then leaned over her.

He leaned over her until his bare chest rested against her back. His heat infused her, scent lured her wolf even closer, and his touch... He didn't stop caressing her clit, the tempo gradually settling in a maddening rhythm. Around and around and around... Jane circled her hips with his ever stroke, fighting for more of that pleasure he gave.

Then he gave her his weight, fingers teasing, body pinning her down and his cock... His cock was a hard brand against her hip, evidence of his need so close to her pussy.

"Are you wet for me, Jane?" he murmured in her ear, his breath fanning her cheek. "Tell me."

"Yes," she whimpered and then whined. Reese slid his fingers along her slit, dipping into her center before returning to her clit again.

"You want my cock, don't you?"

She nodded, but that wasn't enough for him.

"Out loud. Tell me."

Jane shuddered and swallowed, fighting to bring moisture to her mouth. "I want your cock."

"Good girl," he murmured and then nearly made her come right there. He lowered his head and scraped his teeth on her shoulder. He left a searing line of pain in his wake. The kind of pain that merely added to the pleasure.

Her wolf whined with the scratch, wanting more of that delicious ache. It wanted a deeper agony. One that went with being claimed by the dominant wolf. And it didn't give a damn about Jane's plans for the future.

When Reese licked the scratch, Jane was ready to

throw her plans out the window too. Nothing was better than this wolf's mouth, his hands. And as soon as she got his cock, she didn't think anything could be better than that either.

"Spread your legs," he lifted his weight but she could still sense the heaviness of his gaze. "Show me your pussy, now."

She knew he stared at her *there*. His gaze couldn't miss the sight of her asshole and then the entrance to her core.

"Fuck, that's beautiful. So hot, Jane. So sexy." His fingers grazed her opening, taunting her with what was to come. "So mine."

She almost screamed her agreement—begged him to bite and claim her already. But she bit down on her tongue and swallowed the words instead.

"Tell me again." Reese slipped his finger into her core, teasing her sensitize flesh with the simple penetration. "Tell me what you want."

Jane trembled and her pussy clenched around his digit. "I want your cock."

He withdrew and pushed a second finger in. "Not my hand?"

She shook her head and rocked back and forth,

taking what pleasure she could. "Want you to fuck me."

He leaned over her once again, fangs scraping her skin. "Have you ever been fucked by a wolf, Jane?"

She shook her head once again. "Never." He drove his fingers deep, yanking a gasp from her throat. "Never had sex."

Reese froze in place, body immobile, and she didn't think he even bothered to breathe. "You're a virgin?"

The words were all wolf with no hint of his human voice in there at all.

"Yes."

"*Mine*." He rumbled against her shoulder, fangs dancing over her skin once again.

God, she wanted to be his. His and no one else's. But this was a quick one-night stand with a wolf she'd never see again. Her wolf objected to Jane's thoughts but she silenced the beast, too lost in the pleasure to care.

Reese withdrew his fingers, the sudden emptiness yanking a whimper from deep within her chest. But she didn't remain empty for long. A crinkle of foil was soon followed by the feel of the blunt tip of his cock at her entrance.

Condom. He'd gotten a condom. At least one of them had sense.

He was hard and thick, pressed against her virgin entrance. He eased into her, and inch by inch she stretched around his length. A sharp sting joined the pleasure he gave her, the quick pinch of his cock taking her virginity, and her pussy tightened around his shaft. He moved deeper and deeper, not stopping until their hips met and he was buried to the hilt in her core. Her body screamed with need, the desperation for more overriding all thoughts.

"Yes," she hissed. "Now *move*."

In answer, a quick sting jolted over her nerves while the harsh slap of skin on skin filled her ears. Reese smacked her ass again, adding more of the pleasure-tinged pain.

"Ah!" she cried out, but then his hand was back, palm soothing the stinging skin.

"This is my pussy, Jane." He pulled back and popped her again, following it with a soft stroke. "I'll move when I'm ready."

She hoped he was ready soon. Otherwise she'd come from the feel of his hand on her ass and his cock inside her. That seemed to be all her body needed.

Reese repeated the spanking—the spear of pain followed by his gentle touches. Each one drove her closer and closer to release.

Then... then he moved.

He gripped her hips with his large hands, held her steady, and then gradually retreated from her pussy. It was a slow withdrawal followed by an equally slow thrust, a gentle rocking that got her body used to his possession.

At least, that was how it started. Out and then back in again, a sensual glide of their bodies. But soon it changed. Soon he took and gave more.

Soon Reese smacked her ass again while his cock slammed into her pussy. Her pleasure doubled with each strike and she arched her back even more, wordlessly begging him to fucker harder, faster. She wanted the pain that came with his ecstasy and wiggled her ass to get his attention.

And it worked.

Soon they were both covered in sweat, bodies straining for that ultimate peak, that final release that would send them spiraling into utter bliss. The bed shook with his pounding and she clung to the mattress, nails digging into the blanket. She trembled with the bliss of his fucking, the rough and harsh way he claimed her body.

He used her, took what he wanted yet gave her exactly what she needed in return.

Just like their dancing, she'd never felt freer. And as he pushed into her again, she found herself closing her eyes, savoring the feel of his dick as he pushed her to her limits.

"Fuck, *yes*. Your cock feels so fucking good. Gonna..." She tried to talk, but pleasure sucked every breath from her body. Her pussy rippled around Reese's cock, milking his dick with his every move. Heat gathered around her core and slowly spread, the tendrils of ultimate bliss dancing over her nerve endings.

"Come on my cock, Jane. Do it." His nails pricked her hips, slicing into skin and the coppery scent of her blood filled the air.

There were no more words, no more begging and pleading for anything. Reese seemed to read her mind and give her everything she needed. The lewd smack of their bodies increased, his balls slapping against her lower lips and taunting her clit with a hurried caress. She danced closer to the edge of release, the ultimate joy within reach as she let Reese take over her body.

He played her like an instrument, touching and stroking her exactly how she needed most. His fingers found places that drove her wild while his cock stroked her inner walls. She eased to the very tip of the precipice and danced on that sharp point, ready to be tossed over the edge into delirious oblivion.

Reese released a growl of his own, tightening his hold as he pulled her back into his thrusts. He controlled her body, demanding she give in, until she finally relented and let him do as he desired.

She begged and he gave. He demanded and she submitted. He'd push her harder, faster, deeper, and she accepted every snippet of ecstasy that came her way. The knot of need in her stomach tightened further and further, the pleasure gathering and building until she could hardly breathe.

So very, very close...

And then... She lost it. Fire ignited in her veins and raced over her nerve endings, leaving utter joy in its wake. Reese throbbed inside her, his cock pulsing while her core did the same. She milked him for his cum and he gave in, gifting her with his pleasure. He thrust once, twice, and then froze on the third. He sealed their bodies together, hips flush while he continued to ride the wave of his orgasm. Jane rode the wave with him, each roll of pleasure overwhelming all other sensations.

That bliss continued, gradually lessening with each breath until the ecstasy settled into a delicious buzz that she didn't think she'd ever forget. It'd been perfect. More than perfect. It'd been... Hell, she didn't know. She just knew that she couldn't wait to do it again.

And again.

And...

CHAPTER 3

ive months later...

THE SMELL OF BLUEBERRY PANCAKES TURNED JANE'S sensitive stomach, and she took a deep breath, holding it until she thought she'd conquered her nausea. She released it slowly, praying her body would behave long enough for her to eat something. In truth, just about everything made her feel sick these days—everything except for fresh lemonade, orange juice, and anything else remotely citrusy. Hell, she'd even started eating limes like they were apples.

Being pregnant *sucked*. She was always hungry. Of course, everything made her want to puke. Not just food either. The way everyone around the breakfast table looked at her made her want to worship the porcelain god, too.

She'd returned months ago, her dreams of a diploma and a normal life destroyed by a pink plus sign. Then it'd gotten even worse because the entire pack knew of her pregnancy. Not because of some big announcement either. Nope, they all smelled the furry bun in the oven.

They all gawked at her—the alpha's daughter who'd thought she was too good for pack life now running home with her tail between her legs and a stranger's pup in her belly. Of course, no one *said* that, but the sideways glances and snarky whispers made their thoughts pretty obvious.

The humiliation had almost led her to run away again... but that wasn't an option. Shifter babies couldn't control their shift until they hit puberty, which made finding daycare nearly impossible. So, she'd stayed and endured their pointed sniffs, telling her without words they could scent her shame.

Fuck them. The truth of the matter was that she wasn't ashamed. Not of her pup, anyway. If she had to endure their disdain, so be it. No one would ever make her regret her choice, and once the baby came, no one had *better* make her child feel like an outcast. She'd see to that by tooth and claw, if necessary.

Tooth. And. Claw.

"Aren't you going to eat your pancakes, dear?" Her mother's worried voice broke through Jane's thoughts.

"They're, uh…" She swallowed hard and fought not to smell the noxious sweetness of the berries.

Her mother's eyes narrowed slightly, gaze darting between the pancakes and Jane. Jane didn't need to be a mind reader to know what her mother was thinking.

You have to eat. You're eating for two now, sweetheart.

But Ginger Coleman didn't dare say the words aloud. Not in front of her husband, anyway.

Lance Coleman—Jane's dad and pack alpha—glanced at his wife but didn't say a word. He wasn't about to comment on Jane *or* her eating habits—just as he hadn't for months now. He spoke to his daughter only when absolutely necessary.

Which was basically never since he spent most of his time holed up with his enforcers and advisers discussing important pack business while pretending Jane didn't exist. Jane and the bastard pup in her belly. Their disapproval stung. She couldn't deny that, but she would endure it for the sake of her child.

Jane cleared her throat before she spoke again. "I'm not hungry. I'm just going to have some orange juice, I think."

The others sitting around the table glanced her way and then returned to their own conversation as if she didn't exist. Their feigned disinterest didn't banish the tension her presence caused. They treated her like a landmine ready to detonate—avoiding her at all costs and barely acknowledging her existence. If they did, their alpha might be the one to explode, and everyone knew it was just a matter of time. He'd been more and more on edge since she'd moved home.

"You really ought to eat," her mother whispered while she tied her burnished red hair into a knot at the base of her neck. "Just a few bites. For me."

And the baby. Something else her mother didn't say aloud.

Jane sighed and cut into her food as the men pressed on with their conversation.

"He was killed on the border between Coleman and Warren lands." Urgency filled Ian's tone, the younger wolf hurrying to explain more about recent pack happenings.

The determination made sense. They discussed the recent mauling death of Ian's father, after all. Ian's dad, Peter, had been her father's trusted beta for years. Now that he was gone, Ian had recently stepped into his place.

Though, for the life of her, Jane couldn't figure out why.

At least twenty men in the pack had more experience and were more dominant than Ian. Of course, her judgment was probably clouded by the fact that she hated the boy she'd grown up with. Besides, her father probably tapped Ian out of respect for his deceased beta.

"I know where he was found," her father's gruff voice commanded the room.

Jane stared at her father through the curtain of her eyelashes. He hadn't glanced in her direction since she'd come home, so she felt safe in appraising him again. In her youth, Lance Coleman had seemed larger than life. All muscle and sinew and claws and fangs, standing twenty feet tall and roaring with a voice that could be heard around the world. He ruled with a furry iron fist, but he was fair, so his pack trusted and respected him.

Either her memory was faulty, or her father had... shrunk. Because she didn't see a twenty-foot-tall wolf any longer.

Looking at her father, it seemed like nothing could hold back the hands of time. And those hands could be real bitches. Lance looked as if they'd slapped him around quite a bit since Jane had returned. His normally dark blond hair was now mostly grey. Hell, even his skin had a greyish cast. His once massive muscles had seemingly shriveled.

The stress is killing him, Jane thought as she sipped her OJ. *No, I'm killing him.*

"The Warren pack killed my father." Ian's tone transformed from urgent to incensed. "I say we take our revenge."

The pack's enforcers, all meaty brutes who weren't shy about getting physical in the line of duty, grumbled their disagreement. They obviously weren't in favor of Ian's idea. Lance didn't so much as glance their way, his focus on Ian's pale, pinched face.

Icy blue eyes sparkling, Ian clearly saw he had Lance on the hook. The hair on the back of Jane's neck stood on end at how easily he seemed to be manipulating her father. Scooching his chair closer to his alpha, Ian leaned in while he spoke.

"Nobody else but the Warrens had the means or the motive. Everyone in the Coleman pack loved my father, including you. You think it's a coincidence they get a new alpha and my father winds up dead? This Warren alpha is trying to prove his strength to his pack and to us. We need to show him we won't stand for it."

"What do you have in mind?" Lance growled, obviously buying into Ian's theory.

"An ambush."

Ginger gasped and Jane's stomach lurched, and it had nothing to do with the baby growing inside her. Ian shot them both a dirty look and then turned his attention back to her father. He appeared far less shocked than he should have. In fact, he looked almost... eager.

"We have that stupid summit with the new alpha and the National Circle later," Ian continued. "It would be a simple thing for a team to hide in the woods until the Warrens arrive. Then we avenge my father's murder!"

"Hmm..." Lance mused, his expression turning

thoughtful as he actually considered the insane proposition.

A disturbing light shone in Ian's eyes as he smiled at Lance. Jane wanted to smack that grotesque smirk off his face, but even the daughter of the alpha didn't dare attack the pack's beta. Such an act of aggression was grounds for immediate expulsion from the pack, and Jane couldn't risk her unborn child's future like that. But her mother stepped forward, unafraid to defy her alpha's advisor.

"Lance," Ginger said in soothing tones, "you need to keep your word to the National Circle. You agreed to a peaceful meeting of the packs."

"I know what I said," Lance snapped, "but that was before Peter was murdered on the edge of Warren lands!"

Ginger flinched and said nothing. That was so unlike her normally confident and self-possessed mother. It was also out of character for her father to disrespect his mate. Something was going on between them, but Jane was the last person either would confide in. Her mother wouldn't want to burden Jane with their problems, and her father pretty much hated her these days.

"I'll just start cleaning up," Ginger mumbled. Then

she grabbed Jane's untouched food and carried it to the kitchen.

"I need to speak with my enforcers. The study, gentlemen." It wasn't a request. With the creak of his chair, Lance straightened—though he still appeared to be slightly stooped—and disappeared from the room. His grim-faced enforcers followed on his heels.

Which left Jane alone.

With Ian.

Just looking at him made her inner wolf snarl and snap, straining against its leash. They'd known each other since childhood—they'd both been pack royalty—but that didn't mean she liked him. As far as Jane recalled, he was a whiny, sniveling bully who hid behind the pack's enforcers to avoid retaliation. The fact her father selected him as his new beta baffled her.

For a short time, she'd thought maybe he'd changed while she was away at school, but it only took one sleazy come-on to strip her of that notion. Despite the fact his relatively slight build and pale features—including his creepy white-blond hair—held no attraction for her, Ian was relentless in his pursuit of her. It didn't matter that she'd rebuffed his advances for years, the man was persistent.

Now, being alone with him set all her alarm bells clanging.

Clearing her throat, Jane fought to think of an excuse to leave the dining room, but Ian beat her to the punch.

"You know what I don't get?" He stood slowly while his gaze dropped to her baby bump.

A great many things, she desperately wanted to say. Instead, she trained her eyes on her empty juice glass and waited for the inevitable follow-up.

"I don't understand why you won't reveal the name of the baby-daddy. You haven't told your mother or father. Or me." He took two casual steps toward her and then cocked his head questioningly.

The list of answers was limitless, but off the top of her head she could think of a few:

—*Beta or not, you're a weak, worthless asshole.*

—*It's none of your business.*

—*I only know his first name.*

But she kept her mouth shut. In truth, part of her

wondered if she should be grateful to Ian. After all, he was the only person who'd had the balls to ask about the father of her child since she'd come back home. The problem was that he didn't care out of concern for her. He just wanted to satiate his own twisted curiosity. Unfortunately, Jane knew from experience he wouldn't accept any of her answers. Especially the one about him being a weak, worthless asshole.

He took another step toward her, his face shifting into a conspiratorial smile. "There's still time to get rid of it, you know. You could claim you miscarried. Imagine your father's relief! I won't tell anyone, if that's what you're worried about."

Jane's gaze snapped up to his and her upper lip curled in a snarl. One hand dropped to her belly while the other clenched her glass until it cracked. She wondered how hard it would be to clean up the blood if she smashed the glass and cut his throat with one of the sharp shards. Of course, that would mean banishment—if not death. She wouldn't allow her baby to become an orphan.

"I'm not getting rid of my pup," she seethed through clenched teeth as she shot daggers from her eyes.

Why, oh, why couldn't looks kill?

Ian shrugged and edged closer. "You really should

consider it. I'd happily take you as my mate, but not while you're pregnant with a bastard pup. How would it look for the future alpha to raise some other wolf's spawn?"

"Future—" Jane balked and then bit back the fresh wave of outrage as she shook her head. "Thanks for the offer, but... *hard pass*."

A muscle in his jaw flexed at her rudeness, but she didn't care. How dare he think *he'd* be made alpha. *Ever!*

"Everyone's whispering behind your back that it'll be a runt, you know," he sneered, advancing until he stood mere inches from her. "They assume since you won't say who the father is, he must be weak."

She knew he was trying to intimidate her with his size and closeness, but she wasn't about to back down. He might have been slightly stronger than her, but Jane had the power of a mother protecting her child. He'd never survive, and she almost welcomed the chance to prove it.

"They can whisper all they like," Jane spat, giving him a hard look to make sure her next words would pierce that shriveled husk he called a heart. "An alpha's daughter would *never* choose a weak wolf."

Ian growled his displeasure and his eyes clouded

with anger at the implied insult. If she hadn't been so royally pissed off, she would have laughed at him. Tightening her grip on her belly, she bared her teeth, but before either could make the first move, a footstep creaked in the doorway. Ian jumped away in surprise and plastered an innocent smile on his face.

Her father stood in the doorway, staring at Ian. Jane couldn't read his expression, but her heart hoped he was seeing his new beta with fresh eyes.

Her heart hoped wrong.

After a beat, all he said was, "Time to leave for the meeting."

Before he could walk out of the room, Jane called after him. "Can I come?"

It was impulsive and reckless, and she didn't really know why she asked. Except she did. She had to at least *try* to keep him from following Ian's advice and plunging them all into war.

He stopped in his tracks, but his gaze didn't even flick over in her direction. That was nothing new, but then he did something she never expected.

He agreed.

CHAPTER 4

*R*eese let out a heavy sigh and shoved his hands in his pockets. Since arriving at the boundary between pack lands, Brody hadn't quit running his mouth. Reese wasn't sure he was in the mood to listen anymore.

His beta had his—and the pack's—best interests at heart, but nothing he was railing on about was anything Reese hadn't already considered. This meeting, which his father had begged him to set up shortly before his death, had weighed heavily on him since becoming alpha. It was the last step before launching a war nobody wanted.

Reese was, apparently, the only person who could put an end to the madness.

In theory, all he needed to do was get the Colemans to stop encroaching on Warren land. The infringement started not long after the Warren pack's omega diagnosed his father, Jake, with terminal cancer. The Colemans must have found out and decided to push their luck. Their agreement was years old and their sudden violations defied logic. This meeting was because there was only so much pushing Reese would tolerate.

But Reese knew Lance Coleman wouldn't go quietly. The older alpha was stubborn and had a well-earned reputation for his hot temper. When Lance made up his mind about something, there was no changing it. Especially where the Warren pack was concerned. Reese suspected that the moment his father died, Lance had decided to claim all of Wilde Mountain as Coleman land.

No doubt about it, the Warren pack needed to see Reese as a strong leader. But the future stood on a razor's edge —damned if he did, damned if he didn't. Either he made a show of strength, potentially setting off the volatile Coleman alpha, or he looked soft in front of his people in a desperate attempt to make peace. As much as his wolf wanted to show the Colemans just what he was made of, Reese made a promise to his father on his deathbed. A promise he meant to keep.

Always seek peace, his father had whispered to him at the end. He was a shell of the wolf he'd once been, the cancer ravaging his body in a matter of weeks, but his eyes remained alert. It was the pleading expression in his father's eyes that Reese remembered when Brody spoke of going to war. No, he'd remain true to his vow and attempt to keep the peace with the Colemans.

But if that didn't work...

The National Circle, the shifter world's ruling body, would see that it at least held temporarily.

He'd met with the National Circle's alpha, Roman, a few months earlier in Ft. Lauderdale to discuss a transition plan for when his father passed. Now Roman, his beta, Silas, and their enforcer, Dane, were on their way to mediate a meeting that could determine the future of both packs.

"Glad we got here early so they couldn't ambush us," Brody grumbled and then kicked an errant rock on the side of the dusty dirt road. The rock tumbled off the edge of the cliff that overlooked the human town below. "We should have brought enforcers. You know they'll bring some."

"I wouldn't be surprised if they showed up in tanks,"

Reese shot back, growing. He was tired of his beta's grumbling.

"Exactly! We need to show them we have just as much muscle as they have. Intimidation—"

"Intimidation could just piss him off even more," Reese finished. "Lance had an agreement with my father, not with me."

"That's bullshit and you know it. An agreement between packs exists no matter who leads."

"I agree, but my job is to make him understand that, not to get him so riled up he can't hear me." Reese kept his voice measured, doing everything he could to hide his growing tension.

Brody shook his head. "I don't understand how you can be so calm."

Reese chuckled wryly. "You think I'm calm? Every time a Coleman trespasses on our land, my blood boils. It's all I can do to not declare war, but I promised my father I'd pursue peace."

"You've tried. You've turned your cheek so many times, I'm surprised you don't have bruises! They're trying to invade our lands and lay claim to the entire mountain. That's not only a slap in the face to you, but it's an insult to the memory of your father."

"You don't think I know that?" Reese snarled and then took a calming breath. "Father knew tensions would rise after his death. That's why he made me promise."

Jake had also reminded Reese that being a good alpha often meant keeping a level head, even in the face of blatant disrespect. So, he'd forced himself to remain calm. For his father. For his pack.

"I still say we should have brought enforcers," Brody grumbled again.

"The National Circle set the terms, not me. They said no enforcers."

"And nobody has ever defied them?"

Reese brought himself to his full height to remind his best friend who was in charge. "I'm not willing to."

Not yet, anyway.

In his heart, he knew how this meeting would proceed. Roman would do his best to reconcile the two packs, to encourage Lance to accept Reese as the legitimate successor to his father and alpha of this half of Wilde Mountain. Lance would refuse. The man had no trouble breaking a decades-old peace treaty, all but ensuring many from his pack would die in the resulting war. How likely was he to listen to three outsiders who lived far from Wilde Mountain?

But Roman had been clear when he set up this summit. If Lance Coleman refused to back down, Reese would be free to go to war.

His jaw creaked at the thought of wolves dying for no good reason. Their kind weren't so plentiful that either side could afford to waste lives. War would tear both packs to shreds, leaving a hollow victory for the winner. But as much as Reese wanted to prevent that grisly outcome, he wouldn't hesitate to protect his people *or* their land. Just because he wasn't an experienced alpha didn't mean he'd bend over.

The weight of his responsibility weighed heavily on Reese. Every decision he made impacted his pack. If he acted impulsively or chose the wrong path, hundreds of his people could die. Each choice came with its own pros and cons. He just had to predict them all.

No big deal.

"Let's just hope Roman is a skilled negotiator and can talk some sense into Lance," Reese said, checking his watch. Ten more minutes.

"Not likely, considering he thinks you're a murderer."

"Fuck!" Reese punched a nearby tree, allowing himself a moment to release his pent-up frustration. He ignored the pain and struggled to keep a tight rein on his wolf.

Lance Coleman's beta, Peter—an even-tempered guy Reese had always respected—had recently been discovered mauled just a few feet from the border separating their lands. Lance hadn't come right out and accused Reese of the murder, but rumor had it a brown hair had been found at the scene. Damning evidence since the Warren pack were all brunets, while the Colemans were blonds.

"What a crock of horseshit," he groused.

Brody raised an eyebrow. "And that's how you're going to respond when they call you a murderer in front of the National Circle?"

"If that hair had been from one of ours, Lance would have demanded justice immediately. I'm not even sure they *have* a hair. Even if they do, I'll demand testing to prove it's not from a Warren."

"That will still leave the question of who killed the guy," Brody said. "You think Lance had him killed?"

Reese shook his head. "Doesn't make sense. Lance is a hothead, but he's never randomly killed one of his own wolves."

"That we know of..."

Before Reese could respond, the sound of gravel crunching under tires echoed up the road. Two black SUVs with tinted windows trundled up the primitive road, kicking up great plumes of dirt.

Brody planted himself next to Reese and spoke under his breath as he watched the trucks park. "Guess Lance thought it would be a good idea to get here early too."

THE SUV BUMPED ALONG THE UNEVEN DIRT ROAD TO the border. Jane just wished that was the only thing about the ride that was bumpy. Each jolt turned her stomach upside down, and she lingered on the edge of puking for the entire ride.

Of course, her nausea could have been caused by the hate-filled bile spewing from Ian's stupid mouth. From the moment he jumped into the passenger seat, he'd yammered away about vengeance and justice and war. Even the enforcers she was wedged between in the backseat couldn't hide their distaste for the little weasel.

But her father didn't seem bothered in the slightest. In fact, every now and again he'd give a grunt of approval or say something rude about the new Warren alpha. Jane held her tongue and bided her time. She just needed a minute to try and talk him out of doing anything crazy. That wasn't going to be easy, considering he'd barely said two words to her since she'd come home two months earlier. But she sure as hell was going to try.

The car jerked to a stop behind the one carrying even more enforcers. "Dammit, they got here before us!" Ian snarled and then he and the two enforcers bolted from the car to set up a protective perimeter around their alpha. While her father waited for the all-clear signal, Jane saw her chance.

"Daddy?"

He didn't respond, or even acknowledge he heard her, but he tensed up so she knew he was listening. That was as good as she could expect.

"Please don't do this," she pleaded, adding a trembling hint of scared little girl to her voice. She wasn't pretending either. The very thought of a pack war terrified her.

CELIA KYLE & MARINA MADDIX

"Don't do what?" he barked.

Jane pushed through her impulse to cower before her father, her alpha. "Ian's wrong. War won't benefit anyone. Besides, you're a man of your word, and you signed a peace agreement with the Warren pack."

"That agreement was with the Warren alpha."

"And now they have a new alpha," Jane said gently.

Lance snorted. "That kid's no alpha. He couldn't be more than twenty-five, twenty-six tops. He doesn't know the first thing about being a leader. His pack needs me. They just don't know it yet. Now shut your mouth until you can be the alpha bitch I always wanted you to be."

Jane managed to catch a gasp before he heard it. Her father had always been tough, but never cruel. He'd become so aggressive and downright mean recently. He hadn't said a kind word since she'd come home. She couldn't remember him showing her mother any love recently either.

"Land is power, Jane," he barreled on. "You should know that by now."

"Not when you have no claim over it," she shot back.

A low growl rumbled through the car, chilling her

66

blood and setting her wolf to whining. He caught her gaze in the rearview mirror.

"Don't push it. Once Jake Warren died, this entire mountain became Coleman land again—just as it always should have been. If this punk wants it, he's going to have to nut up and fight for it."

Jane held eye contact, a tear spilling down her cheek. "You'd risk your own people—your own *family* —for *land?*"

Her father narrowed his flinty eyes. For the first time, Jane noticed how sunken they seemed, and guilt gnawed at her. This was her fault. She'd disgraced his name, and now he was acting out. He couldn't take his rage out on her, so he was taking it out on *them*.

"You think *he* won't? Besides, it's not just about the land. Do you believe Peter's murderer should go unpunished?"

"Of course not, but I think we should figure out who did it first and not just rely on Ian's best guess."

"What do you know about anything?" He finally tore his gaze away and chuckled derisively. "You couldn't even manage to finish school before getting knocked up with some bastard runt."

"That's enough!"

Jane surprised herself as much as her father with her shout. She'd never defied him so openly before. But alpha or not, no one talked about her baby like that and got away with it.

Lance's eyes grew wide, and for the briefest of moments, Jane thought she saw shame flash in them. Then he turned to the door.

"If you're not willing to stand by your alpha, Jane, stay in the car."

Lance slammed the door shut behind him, leaving Jane in the silence of the car. The baby in her belly kicked harder than she'd ever felt, no doubt in response to her agitation. Rubbing her bump, she tried to calm both her pup *and* her wolf at the same time, even though the chances of doing so were slim. She was simply too amped up and filled with adrenaline.

It seemed as if her father didn't understand a war would affect more than just him. As the alpha, he was deciding the entire pack's future—including her baby's. She refused to raise her child in a world torn apart by violence and hate while her father appeared to be dedicated to that path.

Squaring her shoulders, Jane made a decision. She

was done holding her tongue and allowing her father to bully her. At least *one* of the alphas out there needed to see reason. If it wasn't her father, she'd have to deal with the Warren alpha face to face. Her pack might consider it treason, but they wouldn't be able to stop her. No one would expect it, so she had the element of surprise. The only saving grace was that at least her father hadn't ambushed them as Ian had wanted. Regardless of whether that was by choice or because the Warrens had arrived first, it would give her the chance to plead her case with the Warren alpha.

Opening the door as quietly as she could, Jane slipped out of the SUV and edged along the side until she reached the back of the vehicle the enforcers had driven. Taking a deep, calming breath, she called on all her strength and her wolf's ferocity to see her through the next few minutes. Almost as if in answer, a gust of wind blew a plume of dust into the sky and the trees rustled overhead. The breeze had almost drowned out the sound of two men talking, but the closer she crept, the louder they grew. Sneaking up the far side of the SUV, she tried to peek through the driver-side window but pulled back when she spotted Ian facing her direction.

She took a beat to collect herself, and in that brief moment realized that her father's voice wasn't the only one that sounded familiar. Lance's was brash, commanding, defiant. As always, his harsh tone set her teeth on edge. The other though... It seemed to soothe her frayed nerves.

How can that be?

"The National Circle said no enforcers, Coleman," the deep, rumbling voice reached out for her with invisible hands.

She'd heard it before, but she couldn't quite place it. She'd never so much as met a wolf from the Warren pack, and she knew the wolves in her own. *Who...?* As her brain raced to connect the dots, her heart thumped so loudly in her chest, she was surprised all the wolves in the clearing didn't hear it.

Stepping out from her hiding spot, Jane's gaze zeroed in on the man towering over her father. Muscles flexed and rippled under his tight black t-shirt as he glowered at Lance, a strand of his shaggy brown hair falling in his light brown eyes. Even at a distance, the sun glinted off the gold in them.

Even after so many months of carrying his pup, an intense need washed over her, coating every cell in her body. Memories of how he'd taken control of her and made her scream with pleasure consumed her mind.

She managed another shaky step forward, the crack of a breaking twig drawing everyone's gaze, but she only cared about one. It seemed to take ages to find her voice, and then it came out as barely a whisper.

"Reese?"

CHAPTER 5

*R*eese couldn't believe his eyes. He saw her standing there, but... there was no way she could be there. Right?

Since Lance Coleman had arrived in the clearing— escorted by six massive enforcers—Reese hadn't been able to pinpoint the familiar scent that clung to the man. Coleman's natural aroma nearly overpowered it, but it remained. Like a gentle undercurrent in a warm pool of water. The moment he'd seen the enforcers, Reese's senses had gone into overdrive and his wolf had howled to be released. If it hadn't been for that soothing flavor, he might have obliged—and mostly likely died in the process. But that scent had somehow calmed him enough to control himself.

Then the wind had blown a spiral of dust through the clearing, strengthening the delicious, almost erotic smell. He'd been powerless to breathe it in deeply, memories flooding his confused brain. A hot night in Ft. Lauderdale. A sexy woman with curves that drove him wild. A spray of strawberry blonde hair on his pillow. He hadn't stopped thinking about the stranger for the last five months, but not once had he recalled her aroma at such an inopportune time. He needed to focus, not daydream like a pup with a crush.

With the snap of a twig, his universe flipped upside down in an instant.

Jane stood frozen in front of the black SUV, her eyes wide and her jaw slack. Fuck, she was just as beautiful as he remembered. His wolf rumbled with recognition and strained to be released. It wanted to burst free and take up position in front of her; protect her from the other single males. He wanted to break into a grin and sweep her into his arms, but none of this made sense. He remained in place, unable to think or speak.

Only when her hands wrapped across her belly, almost as if protecting the bump there, did he spot the soft swell. Another gust of wind carried the smell of her mixed with a hint of something else as

73

well. How had he not recognized it? He smelled himself on her. No, not *on* her. *In* her. The truth glowed in her pleading gaze.

The pup she carried was his.

Every ounce of moisture in Reese's mouth evaporated and his heartbeat thundered in his ears. He had so many questions, the first of which was what she was doing there. How had she found him, and why approach him at this completely crazy moment?

Were she and the baby healthy?

The world around him completely forgotten, Reese took a step toward her. "Jane?"

The Coleman alpha blocked him, his big barrel chest bumping into Reese's. Reese tried to sidestep the older wolf to get to Jane, but the asshole kept stepping in his way. Finally, the man snarled and tufts of fur sprouted from various, unattractive parts of him.

"Don't you *dare* speak to my daughter!"

Reese reeled back, unable—unwilling? —to process what Lance Coleman had just said. He stared into the man's furious, crazed eyes, utterly aghast. Jane was his daughter? Jane was a *Coleman*? It wasn't as if their packs did much—okay, *any*—socializing, but how had they not at least seen each other growing up? Surely someone must have known.

Brody. Reese shot a glance to his beta, who simply shrugged.

"I tried to warn you."

Reese swallowed hard. Was that why she'd been in Ft. Lauderdale that night? Had Coleman sent his daughter to seduce him, the enemy of their pack?

He shot her a glance, but couldn't read her expression. Well, he *could*—she looked as confused and excited as he felt—but he wasn't sure if he could trust her. If it had all been a set-up, what was the end game? To compromise him in some way?

The idea she'd been playing him tore his heart to shreds, but that couldn't stop the surge of protectiveness welling inside him. He wanted to believe that need to shield her was really just for the baby, but he couldn't deny the feelings extended to Jane herself. He shook the confusion from his brain and came to a decision. Regardless of whether Jane had betrayed him, there was a baby in the mix now.

Everything else—including his pride—came second.

Glancing around, he wondered if anyone else could

sense what he knew, but either they were blind or they chose to ignore the situation. Lance Coleman looked almost insane, his beta appeared jealous, and their enforcers circled the gathering standing with blank, stony faces.

Reese took another step toward Jane, but her father —her *father!*—stepped in front of him once more. Reese's irritated snarl was matched by a throaty, threatening growl from Lance. Reese realized he was losing control when fur sprouted from his knuckles. Judging by the long hairs sliding down Coleman's nose, the older wolf was losing control, too.

Movement caught Reese's eye. Jane scurried closer to them, her eyes never leaving his, pleading for something. Understanding, perhaps? He didn't know, and right now it didn't matter. Things were going downhill fast.

"Daddy?"

Her voice was a soft symphony, and it boggled Reese's mind that her father ignored her. His gaze remained trained on his opponent, trying to burn him alive with a mere look.

Jane's gaze flicked between Reese and her father. She cleared her throat and tried again. "Daddy..."

"Go back to the car and mind your place," he snarled

without so much as shifting his eyes in her direction. "This is pack business."

A stricken look flashed in Jane's eyes at her father's coldness, and that protectiveness surged inside Reese again. He was about to tell the older man to treat her with the respect the daughter of an alpha deserved, but a slight shake of her head stayed his tongue.

Jane reached a trembling hand out and laid it on Lance's shoulder. "Daddy, listen—"

"Enough!" he roared, spinning around, his arms flailing in blind fury. One hand connected with her cheek, sending her sprawling into the dirt.

The sight of this man, this *father* striking his own daughter would have been enough to send Reese into a rage, but that Lance had knocked down the mother of Reese's child was more than his wolf could bear. Even if he had wanted to salvage anything from this meeting, there was no going back.

Before he could even blink, Reese released his wolf. Normally, he relished the sensation of his arms lengthening and hands melding into great, brown paws, but his sole focus was on the soft spot on Lance's neck that pulsed with his life force. Except, before his shift was complete, Lance began his own transformation into a massive, if aging, sandy-colored beast.

"No!" Jane screamed. "Don't hurt him!"

She scrambled toward the two wolves on her hands and knees, and Reese barked at her. He had no idea which of them she was trying to protect, but he couldn't have her risking their child in a vain attempt to stop the inevitable. Somehow, she understood him and scuttled back the way she'd come, heading for the shaded tree line.

As large as Lance Coleman stood as a wolf, Reese had the physical advantage. Not by much, but enough. They circled each other, foamy drool dripping into the dust at their feet, as they waited for the right moment to attack. Behind Coleman, his beta shifted into a wolf so white he was almost albino and flanked Reese, teeth bared.

Strictly speaking, that was against protocol. When alphas challenged each other, their betas and enforcers stepped back and let the big boys duke it out. But this beta was small and weak. He wouldn't dare attack Reese, and if he did, he'd regret it. The Coleman enforcers glanced at each other nervously, but stayed in their human forms.

Lance must have seen Reese's momentary distraction and took his shot. He lunged, his yellow muzzle snapping and his teeth gnashing. He tried to find purchase on Reese's fur, but Reese was faster. He spun and latched onto the scruff of Lance's neck, a coppery taste filling his mouth.

For a brief moment, Reese thought the altercation was over, that he'd won, but a streak of dark fur knocked him sideways and he lost his grip on the other alpha, who skittered away. Reese regained his footing and saw the cause of the disruption. Brody had tackled the thin, pale beta, who lay struggling mere inches from where Reese had been holding Lance. The bastard had tried to sneak up on Reese from behind.

Fucking Colemans.

He should've known they wouldn't play by the rules —after all, they never really had in all the years their packs remained enemies. Now, lowest of all, their alpha had used his own daughter to confuse Reese's allegiance. Who would send a female to seduce an enemy? An even better question was, who would agree to such a heinous plan?

Reese glanced at Jane again to make sure she was all right in spite of all his suspicions, but the look on her face made him second-guess himself. She could

CELIA KYLE & MARINA MADDIX

have only been scared for her father's safety, but her eyes never wavered from Reese. A warm glow filled him and the truth came into sharp focus.

Jane was faultless. She hadn't been sent by her father to seduce him. They had come together on their own, and now that his head had cleared from the grief of his father's passing, he knew something else. Jane was his mate. Not just because she carried his child, but because it was their fate. After all this nonsense was finished, he'd carry her to his cabin in the woods and claim—

Something barreled into him as he mused, knocking him flat and bringing him back to the present. Lance's muzzle snapped at Reese's neck, his blazing, insane eyes glued to his opponent's jugular, but Reese managed to roll them both to their sides and pull his hind legs up between them.

A switch flipped and a deep, guttural growl rumbled up from deep inside Reese as he kicked at Lance's exposed belly. Each kick was for his unborn child, for his mate, for himself, and each kick grew harder and harder as he vented his rage on the man who had betrayed them all.

He could feel Lance weakening from the assault, and a small voice inside told him to back off, but then the image of the man hitting his own daughter fueled his fury. Suddenly sharp teeth buried deep into his shoulder, drawing a scream of rage and pain from him.

The Coleman beta had broken free from Brody's grip and leapt on Reese, bloodlust glowing in his icy blue eyes. Reese snapped his powerful jaws at the beast and managed to clamp down on an ear. The wolf released his mouthful of Reese and howled in pain. Before Reese could go in for the kill, the white wolf was dragged away. That was followed by strong hands wrapping around Reese's ankle, pulling him from the Coleman alpha.

Writhing around until he could see who dared break up a fight to the death between two alphas, Reese started with surprise. Roman Flynn, alpha of the National Circle, towered over him, his dark brown hair in disarray and his green eyes blazing.

Shit.

Roman's beta, Silas, and enforcer, Dane, guarded Lance Coleman and his whimpering beta. Brody stood behind them, panting and slightly bloodied but looking otherwise unharmed.

"What the *fuck* is going on here!" Roman shouted, commanding everyone's attention and obedience.

Brody shifted back into his human form and stepped

forward. "We got here early so the Colemans couldn't ambush us, and look...they brought six enforcers when you specifically instructed us not to."

Roman shifted his gaze between Reese and Lance. "This meeting was meant to broker peace between your packs. You've both disgraced yourselves and your packs today."

"But they—" Brody tried to object, but Roman cut him off.

"The National Circle will deal with each pack separately, since apparently neither of you are capable of remaining civil or following simple god damned orders. If I get so much as a whiff that either of you have crossed this boundary line, the full wrath of the National Circle will rain down an ungodly fucking firestorm upon you!"

Roman, Silas and Dane stood in a line, arms crossed and scowls warning them all not to cross them. Lance Coleman and his beta shifted back to their human forms and headed for their SUVs. Reese rejoiced internally at their battle scars—especially the devious beta's. His ear hung halfway off his head and blood poured down his neck.

Their enforcers followed, with one gently helping

Jane to her feet. Reese's wolf eyes watched the man's every movement, tensed and ready to attack if he so much as made Jane wince. Reese hated the sight of the man touching her, but with the National Circle standing watch, he couldn't very well do what every fiber of his being screamed to do: tear the enforcer's throat out and drag Jane into the forest so he could claim her as his own. Then they would be a family, and Jane and their pup would be safe forever.

That would come... just not today.

CHAPTER 6

*S*ince the failed peace summit, Jane had spent nearly every minute of the next week in her room. She'd taken all her meals at her desk and spent her days in bed reading, talking to her baby, and trying to figure out her next move.

Jane had been a bit of a pariah before the meeting, but that was nothing compared to how her pack treated her now. When she dared to venture out of her room, only her mother and Ian would look her in eye. Sometimes she'd catch people glaring in her direction, but they'd just turn away and pretend she didn't exist. As far as her pack was concerned, she was persona non grata.

That didn't really bother her. After all, she'd fought

tooth and nail to go to college so she could create a life outside the pack, and everyone had considered her a traitor. But because she was the alpha's daughter, they'd kept their mouths shut. At least until they'd thought she was out of earshot. After the meeting with the Warren alpha—her baby's father—they didn't bother hiding their disdain.

Honestly, she didn't care what any of them thought. Like it or not, she was going to have her baby. The question remained, though, if that baby would have a father.

Reese was never far from her thoughts. As much as she fantasized about him dropping in to see how she was healing, that would be impossible. First, he'd have to fight his way through the entire pack to reach her. A pack who would happily tear him sixteen new assholes. Second, he'd then have to somehow get past her father and his goons. Third, if the National Circle caught wind of such a visit—when they'd forbidden any contact—he'd be stripped of his status and exiled. It was tantamount to a death sentence since wolves needed a pack to survive.

You and your baby need a pack to survive too, a voice whispered in her head.

"Shut up," she mumbled and covered her head with the thick comforter. Unfortunately, she couldn't get away from herself that easily. The voice was right. She needed a pack—that's why she'd returned in the first place—but her own had all but rejected her. No doubt her pup would be even less welcome.

Snuggling into the warm, dark depths of her bed, she daydreamed about moving into Reese's pack. He'd protected her that day, and she knew he'd also been protecting his baby. He either smelled her pregnancy or somehow sensed it, but either way, he knew. No alpha worth the title would allow his pup to be raised without him. He'd come for her, she just knew it, and when he did, she'd live happily ever after as a Warren wolf.

Only...

The truth hit her like a slap in the face. Neither pack would want her *or* her mixed child. The baby would be reviled because of the half of him that didn't belong. The Warrens might be more accepting of her at first, but they'd never trust her. Then, as soon as a towheaded Coleman baby was born, they'd turn on them both, and possibly even Reese. Hugging her tummy, tears burned behind her eyes as she frantically racked her brain for a solution.

A soft knock on her door brought her out from

under the covers. Her mother poked her head in and smiled. Not for the first time, Jane was struck by Ginger's impossible beauty and prayed she'd look half as good at the same age.

"Hi, honey," Ginger said, closing the door gently behind her.

Jane stretched and yawned as she sat up. "What's up?"

"Just thought you'd like some company." Ginger sat beside Jane, cupped her chin, and tipped her face to the side. "Let me see your bruise."

The mark on her cheek had faded to an ugly green, which seemed to satisfy her mother.

"Almost as good as new," Ginger said with a sad smile.

Jane grimaced. "Almost."

"I know I wasn't there, Jane, but—"

"He didn't mean it," Jane finished for her. "Yeah, you've said that already."

"It's not like him to lose control that way." Her mother entwined her fingers with Jane's and stroked the back of her hand.

"It's not like him to snap at you, either," Jane said.

In the past week, the few times she'd heard her father's voice, it had been raised in a gruff shout, calling her mother's name. He didn't ask questions anymore—he made demands—and based on her mother's pained expression, both women knew it was true.

"My relationship with your father is my business," her mother said, and though the words weren't harsh, Jane knew better than to press her further.

"It was bad enough when he didn't look at me," Jane said. "Now he doesn't even talk to me."

On the few occasions they'd found themselves in the same room at the same time, her father had refused to acknowledge her in any way. He'd simply mumble to himself as he hurried out of the room. Sometimes she'd catch a muttered "Warren" or "bitch," and even though she pretended not to hear, her heart always folded in on itself just a little more.

"He could be feeling guilty about what he did," Ginger offered. "People react differently when they know they were in the wrong. Your father is no different. He's a proud man."

"It's not just him, Mom."

Ginger frowned. "Who?"

"Everyone!" Jane huffed as she climbed out of bed and moved to the window.

The front of her pajama bottoms rolled down to settle under her pregnancy bump, reminding her it was time to go shopping for maternity clothes. *If* she could manage to drag herself out of her room.

"They hate me, Mom. They hated that I came home knocked up by some strange wolf. Now word has spread like wildfire that Reese and I recognized each other. So, of course, they hate me even more. What's worse is they'll hate my baby."

Ginger moved to her daughter and enfolded her in a comforting embrace. They stood that way for some time, swaying gently as Jane knew she'd sway with her own child when he or she needed the comfort only a mother could give.

"I should have known my daughter would choose an alpha," Ginger finally murmured into Jane's hair.

"Even if it's the wrong alpha?"

"Who says?" Ginger demanded, pushing her daughter to arm's length. "A baby that is both Warren and Coleman? That will be a fearsome wolf, my dearest. Strong too. Maybe strong enough to unite both clans once and for all. A union between you and the Warren alpha..."

"Nobody said anything about a *union*. He didn't claim me. As far as I know, he hasn't given my condition a second thought."

Jane knew she was pouting, but sometimes a girl just needed a good pout. Of course, her mother would never let her wallow.

"I hardly think he's had the chance with you locked away like a princess in a tower."

Jane sighed heavily. "I know, I just..."

"You miss him?"

She did. All these months, even before she discovered she was pregnant, she'd longed for Reese. She ached for him to hold her one more time, to kiss her so hard her toes curled, then make love to her until she screamed. She'd made her peace that she'd never see him again, but then... There he was. And he lived just a few miles away, yet it might as well have been a million.

Tired of thinking about the mate she could never have, Jane changed subjects.

"I'm worried about Daddy."

Her mother stiffened but remained silent.

"Don't you think he's been different lately?" Jane pressed.

Ginger released Jane and smoothed her auburn locks away from her face. "I think he's under a lot of stress. You know how close he was with Peter. The death of a beta can be hard on an alpha."

"It seems like more than that, Mom. I've caught him talking to himself a lot lately. And he's—" Jane shook her head, trying to find the word. "—*cruel*. He calls me names under his breath and he's unforgivably rude to you. I'm starting to wonder if something is seriously wrong."

A gentle crease appeared between her mother's eyes, but that was all the other woman gave away. "Like I said, your father is under a lot of stress, and that's the last word I have on the subject, understand?"

"Yes, ma'am," Jane demurred.

Of course, not talking didn't make her concerns vanish. Jane worried what would happen if her father really was sick. If he died or turned feral, Ian would be next in line to become alpha. A chill rippled down her spine and raised goosebumps over her entire body.

Ginger pulled Jane into a quick hug. "Well, my dearest, what can I get you for dinner?"

"Dinner?" Jane said with a laugh.

Ginger raised a solitary eyebrow. "It's almost six."

"Oh." Time certainly flew by when one hid under the covers all damn day. "I'm not hungry. Maybe some—"

"Orange juice?" Her mother shook her head. "I'll bring you food, too. See that you eat it. A baby of such strong lineage will need everything you can give it."

With another gentle smile, Ginger swept from the room, leaving the door ajar behind her.

Jane stared blankly at the door, willing herself to close it before her father stalked past and cursed her again. Then again, maybe she ought to go for a run —a nice long one to clear her mind and get her thinking straight again. The enforcers would no doubt follow her, but she'd make them work for it. Even five months pregnant, she was fast.

The challenge of humiliating the enforcers boosted her spirits enough to dig out her running clothes. She was just about to drop her PJ bottoms when the door creaked open behind her. Ginger must have already had a meal prepared. Always the mother hen, and Jane wouldn't have it any other way.

"That was fa—"

Jane's smile quickly turned into a grimace. Ian stood in the doorway, biting his lip and letting his nasty gaze slide up and down her body. *And now I need a shower.*

"Get out of here, Ian. This is my private bedroom."

She glared at him with all the hatefire burning inside her. He smiled in return.

"I thought a private room would be best for a *private* conversation."

He swung the door shut behind him, the soft click seeming to echo through the quiet room. He slunk toward her and took a seat on Jane's mussed bed. Her upper lip peeled back in a snarl that he'd dare get so close to where she slept. The slimy smirk never left his pinched, smug face.

"Haven't seen you at all this week," he finally said, his tone smooth, as if he actually gave a rat's ass.

Ever think that was by design, asshole? She didn't dare say that though.

"I've been right here." Even though her voice was a perfect monotone, she could still hear the edge of disgust rimming her words.

Ice shimmered in his leer. "That doesn't mean you've been present, does it? I haven't seen you on runs or at meals."

Jane cocked an eyebrow at him. "So, you're here because you missed me?"

The corner of his lip raised in what she could only guess was mock amusement. It certainly wasn't what anyone in the world would consider a smile.

"Maybe. But I also think it's important for you to know what's going on. And what will come next."

Jane frowned and crossed her arms, preparing herself for whatever bullshit Ian was about to spew.

"Your father is losing control of the pack," Ian said dispassionately. "His thirst for war is weakening the people's devotion. It's understandable. They don't want their sons and daughters to die in a pointless war."

"War was your idea!" The balls on this guy!

Ian waved her comment away like an annoying gnat. "Regardless, your father's days are numbered. After he's gone—one way or another—*I* will become alpha."

It was almost as if he'd read her mind from earlier.

She'd brushed away her thoughts, telling herself she was just being paranoid, but now he was here confirming her suspicions.

"You came to threaten me?" Jane spat.

"I'm not threatening you, Jane," Ian said, his voice oozing with what he probably thought was charm. "I came to give you a choice."

Jane glowered but remained silent.

"When your father dies at the hands of my followers, you can die alongside him and your mother or..."

A rage like none Jane had ever felt grew inside her. It was only matched by fear. Fear for herself, her parents, but most of all, her child.

"Or give up my baby and allow you to take me as your mate?"

Ian stood and brushed imaginary lint from his pants. When he finally met her gaze, the fear in Jane's heart turned to horror.

"The baby won't live either way, Jane. You can save yourself, though. There will be other pups. Pups born of a worthy father."

"And exactly how do you expect me to answer?"

Ian chuckled. "Oh, I already know your answer. I'm proving what a generous alpha I'll be by giving you one last chance to change your mind."

Ian left her standing there, mouth gaping in shock, and slammed the door on his way out. Her wolf strained to be set free so she could tear the little asshole to shreds, but she remained frozen in place, completely paralyzed.

Ian wasn't wrong. Her father *was* losing control of the pack, not to mention his mind. If she told him about Ian's threat... He'd never believe *her*, of all people.

Jane's worst fears had been confirmed by the very man she feared the most. This was no longer her pack, and if she was honest with herself, it hadn't been for a very long time. There was only one thing she could do—run. Run far and fast to somewhere her baby would be safe. She had to escape, the only question was where to go.

Except, there really was no question. She had to find Reese. Somehow. She knew in her gut that he'd protect her and their pup. The real question was if he would also protect her family. As determined as she was to save her child, she couldn't just leave her parents to die at the hands of that foul piece of shit.

She would need Reese's help. But the last time she'd seen him, he hadn't looked to be in a forgiving mood.

CHAPTER 7

*R*eese bounded through the dark forest, branches slapping at his muzzle as he fought to outrun his demons. He barely felt the whip of fast scratches through his fur and flesh. He needed the run. More than that, his wolf needed the physical activity. Both halves of him had to burn off some of the confusion, frustration, and anger that'd been eating at him since the botched summit.

After the fight with the Colemans, Roman and the other members of the National Circle had formally reprimanded him for his behavior. They'd promised Lance Coleman and his beta would also be chastised. *Right.* Reese silently wondered what effect that might have on a couple of lunatics.

Reese's wolf had become frantic the moment Jane

had climbed back into that black-as-death SUV. He didn't miss the way her gaze sought him out and then she was gone—the door closed and tinted windows hiding her from his view. His beast had howled in protest as the truck carrying her drove off. Reese had summoned every ounce of strength he possessed not to chase after it like a stupid dog on the street. Instead, he'd waited until the dust had settled and then he'd run into the forest, full throttle.

He'd been running ever since.

His wolf demanded he hunt down their mate and pup, but Reese had to tread carefully. As much as he yearned to slaughter any Coleman who dared to stand between him and his new family, he'd made a promise to his dying father to seek peace at all costs. On top of that, he sensed something... *off* with Lance Coleman.

Naturally, Jane's unexpected pregnancy had no doubt rocked their pack to the core, but something else swam just under the surface. Something dark and evil. He simply didn't know what it might be. If he could somehow track her down, maybe he could figure it out and find a solution.

No, it was too dangerous—not just for him, but for Jane as well—to invade Coleman lands. They no doubt had sentries protecting the border, and getting caught meant certain death. That didn't stop him from trying to come up with a safer solution, though. He had so many questions, not the least of which was if she'd set him up.

A growl bounced off the trees, sending a jolt of adrenaline rushing through his body. It took a moment to realize his wolf had been growling at *him* for thinking his mate would betray him in such a way. And in his heart, he knew the truth. Fate had brought them together for one incredible night to heal the wounds between their packs. He just had to make sure they all survived to see it through to the end.

Even a passing thought about their night together in Ft. Lauderdale brought back a flood of memories. He tried to push them away, but it was no use. Even as he sprinted through the woods, he couldn't outrun his memories. They'd become part of the fabric of his soul.

Jane dancing with him, grinding her luscious ass into him until he couldn't control himself. The feel of her full lips wrapping around his cock. The way her hips arched into him as he rocked into her, begging him to go even deeper.

Fuck.

He shoved the vivid memories from his brain. It wouldn't do for one of his pack to see their alpha in wolf form running around with a boner. The very thought took care of the problem in a heartbeat.

His paws were caked with mud and his muscles burned by the time he reached his small cabin near the boundary line. If that hadn't run the piss and vinegar out of his wolf, nothing would. Panting heavily in the crisp night air, he pulled his beast back, stretching his arms and rolling his shoulders as fur shifted to skin.

An evening alone, away from the pressures of being alpha, might allow him the quiet he needed to plan his next move. His pack was understandably skittish, thinking they were on the brink of war. No amount of reassurance from him could soothe them— probably because they could smell his own agitation. Unfortunately, living in the pack house didn't offer a lot of privacy. The only place for him to be alone was his tiny, private man-cave out in the middle of nowhere.

His skin erupted in goosebumps as he mounted the steps and let himself inside. Fall felt heavy in the air around him, so his first stop was a small cardboard box that held spare clothes. Shrugging a hoodie over his head and tugging on some sweatpants, he then piled some kindling in the little potbelly stove in the middle of the one-room cabin. Except, before he could light the match, a loud howl ripped through the night. He'd recognize that call anywhere—an enforcer needed backup.

Damn.

Reese's cabin sat just a few hundred yards from Coleman lands, so it stood to reason another Coleman enforcer had tried pushing onto Warren land again. As much as he'd like to let his men tear out the throat of the intruder, that wasn't the path to peace. He picked up his pace to make sure he reached the scene before anything happened.

Normally, he'd shift back into his wolf form for the boost in speed, but the call sounded close. Very close. Pausing to shift would only slow him down.

Plus, he didn't want to ruin another set of clothes over a Coleman.

He caught the scent on the air before the scene came into view. A wall of Warren scents hit him full force. Several of his sentries in wolf form stood in a circle, growling and gnashing their teeth at the trespasser. The moon had yet to rise, so Reese couldn't see the Coleman in question, but an aroma eventually wound its way through the testosterone and body odor. When the faint flavors reached him, he pushed past furry bodies to confirm what his wolf already knew.

Jane stood in the center of the circle, her strawberry blonde hair pulled into a ponytail and a backpack slung across her back. She held two enormous hunting knives and glared at each wolf in turn, her eyes wild with a combination of fear and fury. It was almost as if she dared them to make the first move.

She didn't have to wait long. Ren, one of their best enforcers, sprang forward and lunged for Jane's throat. She sidestepped him deftly and swiped one knife through the air, slashing Ren's haunch. The enforcer crumpled to the ground a bleeding, whining wreck.

Pride like Reese had never felt swelled inside him for his mate's bravery. She truly was an alpha bitch to her very core. He almost wanted to see how she'd handle the rest of his pack, but he couldn't stomach the idea of her getting hurt—or worse. As the other wolves inched closer, Reese pushed his way past furry bodies to stand at her side.

"Back off!" he shouted, his tone firm.

The circle of wolves paused mid-step, some glancing at each other in confusion while a few whined.

Regardless, they all backed away, giving their alpha and the Coleman spy space. They no doubt assumed Reese wanted the honor of killing her.

Instead, he wrapped a steadying arm around her trembling shoulders. When her pale green gaze latched onto his, he almost forgot anyone else in the world existed.

"Reese!" An angry voice cut through the fog in his brain. A young sentry named Declan had shifted to get to the bottom of the matter.

"What is it, Declan?" Reese kept his tone even and calm.

Declan stared at him, mouth hanging open, as if the answer to the question was obvious. He raised his hands and looked incredulous, totally speechless. Finally, he managed a lame, "What the fuck?"

Jane tensed next to him, but Reese remained calm. "Would you like to rephrase your question, Declan?"

Declan's face burned red. "This is bullshit! That Coleman bitch just walks right onto Warren land and you're going to let her go free? We should send her back to her daddy in pieces to send those bastards a message!"

Reese's facade of composure crumbled at the threat

to his mate and his pup. He allowed his wolf to show a little of itself as he snarled at the upstart sentry.

"You so much as *look* at her the wrong way, and you'll be the one who ends up in pieces, boy. This is none of your business."

"That bastard she's carrying is *all* of our business," Declan sneered. He sniffed the air for effect. "As if we can't smell it on her."

The young man had grown up with Jake Warren as alpha, and perhaps he resented the fact Reese took his father's place. Or maybe he was testing the new alpha's boundaries.

Or maybe he was just stupid.

Declan looked to the other wolves for approval, all of whom avoided his gaze. Turning back to Reese, he glared at them both.

"It's unnatural and you should get rid of it as soon as possible before any more damage is done!"

Confirmed. The kid was stupid. He needed to be taught a lesson—they all did—and Reese was happy to oblige. Before Declan could raise his hands to defend himself, Reese was on him, smashing his fist into Declan's face. The sentry bounced off a nearby

CELIA KYLE & MARINA MADDIX

tree from the force and fell to the spongy earth in a heap.

Reese hadn't come close to giving the man everything he deserved, but killing one of his own would only make things worse. Instead, he shoved Declan with his foot until he lay face up, blood pouring from his broken nose. He coughed up a spray of blood before meeting Reese's gaze. Reese crouched next to him, hands on his knees as he peered into terrified eyes.

"Will you submit to me, your alpha, or should we make this more interesting?"

Tears of pain mixed with Declan's blood as he shook his head frantically. "I thubmit! I thubmit!"

Reese gave him a stiff nod and reached out a hand. Declan winced, thinking Reese was going to hit him again, but quickly realized his alpha was offering him a hand up. Once the kid was steady on his feet, Reese slapped him on the back—perhaps a little harder than was strictly necessary—and made his way back to Jane's side.

"Go home," he commanded. "I'll hear nothing more on this matter."

He watched as each wolf disappeared into the blackness of the trees, Ren limping and Declan holding his bloody nose. Not a single one so much as looked over their shoulder.

"Thank you," Jane whispered.

When he was sure all of his men had followed his orders, he turned to her and gathered her into his arms. He still had a thousand questions, but right now, he just needed to hold her, to prove to himself she and their baby were fine.

"What for?" he asked gently.

"For saving my life. There were so many..."

Reese smiled. "And you showed them what you're made of."

She searched his face, looking for reassurance or acceptance or... something. He wanted to give that to her and more, but first things first.

"It was foolhardy to come here like that," he said, trying not to sound too scolding. She'd had a hell of a night already. "You're carrying our baby. You need to be more careful."

Her eyes grew wide and then filled with tears. "You knew."

It wasn't a question. Of course it wasn't. They were connected now on a cellular level. All that was left was to claim her as his mate, and as much as he wanted to do that right there on the forest floor, Jane needed to rest.

"Just promise me you'll be more careful," he said as he stooped to pick her up. Alarm shot through him at how light she felt in his arms. Like a starving bird.

"I promise," she whispered into his chest as she nestled in. "I didn't have a choice though. Reese, I need your help."

"You'll have it, Jane, but first you need some sleep. We can talk about everything in the morning."

Within three paces, Jane's breathing slowed and her body went limp. She barely moved when he finally tucked her into his small bunk in the cabin. As he sat by the fire watching the shadows flicker on her beautiful face, a sense of wonder and gratitude nearly overwhelmed him. Gratitude for finding her before she was killed by his men, gratitude for their baby, but most of all gratitude that they were finally under his protection.

They were home.

CHAPTER 8

*J*ane wasn't sure what woke her—the pop and sizzle of bacon cooking or the tantalizing scent. Whichever it was, her stomach growled in anticipation of shoveling about a hundred strips of crispy, fatty goodness into her mouth.

Damn, she hadn't felt hungry for months, but she was pretty sure she could scarf down a greasy mountain of meat. Eggs and some French toast would hit the spot too. Maybe an omelet and a waffle. *Definitely* some sausage and pancakes. Then she'd wash it all down with a big glass of orange juice. Not one of those miniscule juice glasses restaurants used, but a big fat water glass brimming with the good stuff.

Cracking open one eye to the brightness of morning, her gazed drifted to Reese's very broad, very shirtless back as he stood at a little wood-burning stove. A hot, sexy alpha who *cooked*? All her dreams had just come true!

The bed creaked underneath her as she rolled onto her back and stretched. She hadn't slept so well in months, maybe years. And it wasn't like the mattress could claim the credit. It was barely a notch above the crappy old futon in her college apartment.

Reese immediately dropped his spatula and rushed to her. "Are you okay? Is the baby?"

Jane couldn't resist reaching up and letting her fingers skitter down his cheek to his stubbly jawline. She'd often dreamed about touching him again since that fateful night, but not once had it been of caressing his face!

"We're fine," she murmured, willing him to dip down and kiss her. "Don't worry. Go back to your cooking."

Jane could see the conflict in his eyes. He wanted to kiss her as much as she wanted it, but now wasn't the time.

"We need to talk," he finally grated out.

Jane grimaced. "I know, but only if there's food involved."

Reese blinked and then smiled. "Fair enough. Bacon's done. How much do you want?"

"I only want one piece," Jane said, smirking as her stomach rumbled. "Our baby, on the other hand, wants it all."

He laughed as he stood. "My pup gets what he wants."

"Or she," she noted as he went to fetch some grub.

Jane couldn't remember a thing after Reese had picked her up in his arms after she'd tried fighting off a pack of Warren enforcers in her human form. He'd been right that it wasn't her best idea, but Ian had given her no choice. She either ran and took the risk of being killed, or she stayed and guaranteed not only her death, but her baby's and her parents'. It was the easiest decision she'd ever made.

Sitting up as Reese piled a plate high with bacon, she took in her surroundings. They were in a small, one-room log cabin, newly built by the looks of it. Oil lamps were scattered about, and every stick of furniture looked to have been handmade out of hand-harvested branches and logs. It wasn't luxurious by any stretch of the imagination, but it was warm and cozy, and had clearly been built with love.

"Do you live here?"

"No," Reese said, smiling as he sat on the edge of the small bed and put the plate between them. "I live in the pack house. I built this after my father died. I use it when I need some alone time."

"Really?" Jane said through a mouthful of bacon.

"When my father was diagnosed with cancer, everyone turned to me for guidance. I would be the new alpha, after all. So not only was I dealing with my changing role in the pack, but I was also caring for my father during his final days. I needed a place to think without a thousand voices yammering away at me."

"I'm sorry about your father, Reese. Truly."

She laid a comforting hand on his. He looked down at it and then entwined his fingers in hers.

"Thank you. But we should be discussing our... situation."

"Whatever could you be talking about?" she asked innocently before shoving three more pieces of bacon in her mouth.

Reese smiled, despite the gravity of their "situation."

"First things first," he said, hooking a finger under her chin and tipping her head to the side so he could inspect her fading bruise. "It's healing nicely."

At the light touch, a thrill sizzled from her chin to her very core. Swallowing hard, she nodded. "I'm a lot tougher than I look."

"I can see that. You're also impulsive to the point of being reckless. What were you thinking crossing the border in the middle of the night like that? If I hadn't been near…"

Jane's cheeks grew warm at being chastised, but she knew where he was coming from. "It was dangerous, but not reckless. Either I tried to find you, or I faced certain death."

A rumble echoed through the cabin before Jane realized it was coming from inside Reese. His upper lip quivered and his eyes blazed with anger.

"Tell me everything."

Jane hesitated in telling him *everything*. He was no more than a stranger to her, really, and she had no idea how he'd react. The last thing she wanted was for her baby's father to go charging into Coleman lands in a fit of rage. So, she started slowly.

"I never really felt like I belonged to my pack. My father is overbearing and very old-school. There was never any room for discussion with him. I had to do as he said or face the consequences, even in matters as trivial as what clothes I was allowed to wear. I never felt as if I could just be me. He didn't just overshadow me; he *eclipsed* me."

She popped another piece of bacon in her mouth and chewed deliberately as she tried to figure out how to continue. Reese sat patiently, watching her intently, devoid of judgment or expectations. No one had ever looked at her like that before, and not just because her father was the alpha of their pack.

"My father's always been domineering, that's true, but ever since I came home, he's been...*different*." She shrugged and dropped her gaze. "I don't know, maybe it's just the shame of his daughter getting knocked up and dropping out of school."

Reese frowned. "School?"

His question drove home the fact they knew next to nothing about each other. But somehow, that didn't seem to matter to her heart. Now that they were together, the connection between them grew stronger than ever.

"Yes, I left the pack to go to college."

"With... *humans?*" He looked scandalized.

Jane smiled. "Yup. They're actually not that bad. Most of the time. Of course, none of them knew the truth about me. In fact, that was the whole point."

"I don't understand."

"Turns out, neither did I. You see, I thought that since I never felt at home in my own pack, I might find a place out in the human world. It took *forever* to talk my father into letting me go, and it was mostly my mother's doing, but what I never admitted to anyone was that my secret goal was to assimilate."

Reese shook his head. "Aside from the obvious risk of being discovered, a wolf without a pack will almost certainly turn feral and go mad. What made you think you'd be any different?"

Jane shrugged. "I was young and stupid and thought I'd be different. It turns out what I really wanted wasn't to become a human at all. I was willing to make the sacrifice of denying my true nature for the chance to live life on my own terms. I simply didn't want to live under my father's thumb anymore."

"So why did you return?" Reese asked, looking honestly puzzled.

Jane's eyebrow shot up and she tilted her head. "Really?"

He continued to appear confused until her hand drifted down to her tummy.

"Oh, right."

"Yup, one crazy night on spring break, and I turn up preggers. Imagine my dad's delight." She sniffed, trying to pass it off as a joke when it was anything but. "Anyway, no way could I live a normal human life with a shifter baby. It's not like I could hide him away until he hit puberty and was finally able to control his shift. Of course, I had no idea who or where you were, so I scurried home with my tail between my legs."

"So..." he started but then stopped. His gaze grew even more intense, which Jane would have bet was impossible. "You didn't know who I was?"

Jane frowned and then understanding dawned. "Are you asking if I set you up? If my father forced me to seduce you so he could gain some bizarre upper hand and take control of your lands?"

At least he had the grace to blush. "I'm sorry."

Her heart swelled at the contrite expression clouding his chiseled features. Pulling his hand to her belly, she smiled. "Don't be. Whatever has happened, or will happen, I will never regret our night together because it led to this."

Silence stretched between them, their hands locked together on the baby they'd made. Jane hadn't known it then, but her life had changed forever that night, and she wouldn't change a single thing.

"I wish I'd known," Reese said, his voice tinged with regret but not incrimination.

"I wish I could have told you."

His gold-flecked eyes locked onto hers. "I've missed so much."

"Mostly a lot of throwing up," Jane said, laughing. "And orange juice."

"Orange juice?"

"Cravings are intense."

Reese finally smiled. "I'll buy five gallons tomorrow. And I'll make sure the freezer is stocked with bacon."

He twisted his fingers around hers, and though the intimate gesture should have felt foreign or forced, it didn't. Not to her. The warmth of his skin spread through her like a comforting embrace.

"From now on, you won't have to go through any of this alone," he said, squeezing her hand. "I'll be with you every step of the way."

Jane wanted nothing more in that moment than to lean forward and kiss Reese. But if she did that, they'd be busy for at least an hour—hopefully more —and they had more to discuss. It couldn't wait.

"That's good to hear because you're the only one who can save my family."

"What do you mean?" Reese asked, concern flashing across his face.

This was why she'd sought him out, but now that the moment had arrived, she struggled to find the words. Once she told Reese the full story, *his* life might be in danger. But he needed to know.

"First, it's my turn to ask you an awkward question. Did you murder my father's beta?"

"Of course not!" Reese tried to yank his hand away, but Jane kept a tight grip on it.

"I didn't think so," she said, calming him instantly. "Ian, the new beta, is an evil bastard who needs to die."

Reese didn't balk or even so much as blink. He just asked, "Why?"

"He's been whispering into my father's ear that a war with the Warren pack was the only option. My father's erratic behavior made manipulating him easy, but now that the two packs are on the brink, he's changed his tune. Says he's going to overthrow my father with his followers."

Reese scowled, chewing on this bit of information. "A green beta pushing out his alpha? That's not how it works."

"He's not only pushing my father out, he point blank told me he plans to execute both of my parents, and..."

"And what?" Reese asked, noticing her hesitation.

"And me, if I don't get rid of my baby and become his mate."

The bed lurched when Reese jumped up and seemed to grow taller than she remembered. Fur sprouted from his knuckles and his teeth grew long enough to protrude from his mouth. His deep, throaty growl bounced off the walls of the little cabin, and her wolf joined in.

"You're mine," he snarled, fire blazing in his eyes.

Far from feeling threatened, a sense of peace and security enveloped Jane. In the face of such ferocity from a true alpha—not a wannabe—Ian's threats seemed like a pathetic joke. Just like Ian.

"No one will *ever* hurt you again, Jane. I need you to know that. *Never!*"

Jane moved onto her knees and pressed her cheek against his chest, listening to the thunder inside. "I know," she whispered.

Reese wrapped her in a protective hug, and Jane thought she could have stayed like that forever. Until he tipped her head back and stared deep into her eyes. In that moment, she knew he was ready to claim her—and she was ready to be claimed.

"And I won't let anything happen to your parents either. I don't know what's wrong with your father, but I'm going to find out. Right after I take you as my own so there's no question about your allegiance."

Jane had already begun skimming her hands along the hard planes of his body. She smiled up at him and grabbed two handfuls of the sweetest ass she'd ever seen.

"Quit talking and do it already."

CHAPTER 9

*R*eese's inner wolf gnawed and clawed at him, begged him to claim Jane as his own. Now.

Her soft curves flush with his chest were almost too much for him to bear, her silken skin beckoning him and almost begging for his touch. Her warm breath fanned across his skin, her sweet scent filling his nose and straining his control even further. He stroked her hair and fought for calm, reminding himself of what she'd gone through last night. She'd suffered to reach him and claiming her now would be physically exhausting. She was pregnant with his pup and should rest.

Unfortunately, his cock—and his wolf—disagreed. Blood raced to his dick, his shaft filling and lengthening until he throbbed with want. His wolf nudged and prodded him, reminding him of her creamy skin and how good she'd tasted—how good it'd felt when she came on his cock. His balls drew up tight, aching and heavy between his legs. He'd sink into her over and over again until...

Jane sighed and shifted her weight from one leg to another, turning her head to nuzzle his neck. He wondered if she knew what her scent did to him, how her nearness affected his body and soul. Not just her nearness. *Their* nearness. He slid his hand down until he cupped the roundness of her stomach, the warm haven where his pup rested inside her. The reality of the situation—his new future—suffused him. No matter what happened outside this cabin, he and Jane were going to have a baby.

And if Jane was any indication of how their kid would turn out... he was going to be a fighter. Smiling, he slid his hand lower only to feel a gentle nudge against his palm.

Reese gasped and looked down to where his palm lay. Then he shifted his attention to Jane. "Did you feel that?"

"Of course." Jane released a tinkling laugh. "I'm the one getting kicked."

He dropped to his knees and cupped her stomach with both hands, aching to feel the nudge of his pup again. He wanted—needed—the baby to know that Daddy was there and wouldn't leave him alone again.

"Incredible," he whispered.

He'd already missed so much, but he refused to miss another moment.

He carefully turned his head and rested his ear on Jane's tummy, listening to the sounds inside her. It could have been his imagination, his expectations projecting what he desperately sought, but he was sure he heard a rapid heartbeat.

This was his baby—their baby.

And he would do anything to keep them safe.

Closing his eyes, he pressed a kiss just above Jane's belly button and then below it, a silent thanks for what she was giving him.

She giggled. "What are you doing?"

Reese ignored her and tugged on her shirt, lifting it to expose her pale skin. He brushed his lips over the swell of her stomach, breathing in her natural scent. Not just *hers*. No, there was a mixture of their flavors tinging her natural aroma. He rubbed his cheek against her skin, imagining himself nuzzling their child. If his calculations were correct, Jane was about halfway through her pregnancy, which meant he'd get to meet his pup soon.

But not soon enough as far as he was concerned.

Reese eased back and met Jane's stare, her lips holding the smallest of smiles while confusion filled her eyes. "You're incredible. Did you know that?"

She shook her head, another laugh escaping her lips. "I'm an incubator."

"No, you're so much more. You... you glow, Jane. You're so beautiful you take my breath away." He shook his head and then kissed her stomach once more. He breathed deeply, searching for their combined scent, but found something else there, too. The flavors of Jane's desire taunted him, the musky sweet scent of her need drawing his wolf forward. His next kiss was even lower, closer to that delicious part of her and she squirmed with his attentions.

"Reese..."

He murmured against her flesh, speaking between sensual kisses. "I don't regret a damn thing. I want you to know that." He scraped his fangs across her hip. He remembered she loved feeling his teeth.

"You and this baby are everything." He licked away the sting and met her gaze again. "Everything."

Jane blinked and swallowed hard. "Me too."

"Will you let me show you? Let me show you what you mean to me?"

"What?" Jane whispered.

"Want to take my time. Want to show you how much I lo—How much I want you. We've fucked, but I want more for our mating. If you're too tired—"

"I'm not." Jane rushed out the words. "I already told you I want to be yours."

"Good." He grinned and reached for her jeans, sliding his thumbs in the belt loops and giving them a tug without fussing with the zipper. The fabric easily slid down her legs to pool at her feet.

While he worked, Jane pulled on her shirt, whipping it over her head. The whoosh of her shallow breathing told him more than words. She ached for this, anticipated the pleasure he could—would—give her. The thrum of her heartbeat hit double time when he reached for the edge of her panties. He pulled those away, too, revealing the prettiest pussy he'd ever seen.

Memories of their one night together flickered

CELIA KYLE & MARINA MADDIX

through his mind, the salty sweet taste of her arousal one of the highlights of the evening.

"God, you're gorgeous," Reese breathed and then leaned forward. He pressed gentle kisses to her thigh, nuzzling and nudging her to spread her legs. She eased them apart for him, giving him access to the pink flushed part of her he craved. He sucked on her skin, teased her with his fangs, and tasted every bit of her he could reach. His wolf growled in satisfaction, nudging and pushing him to move on with the claiming. It wanted to release his fangs and bite his mate, take her quickly before she could change her mind.

Tempting, but he would show her all he had to offer —everything she could expect for the rest of their lives. Reese wasn't a one-minute man and he would remind her of that fact.

He switched his sensual kisses to her other leg, teasing before returning to his slow, careful trail up her thigh. He drew closer to his destination, her closely cropped curls teasing his nose, and he nudged her to step back.

"Sit. Need to taste you." He hoped she understood his words since his voice held more than a hint of his wolf.

Jane eased to the cushions and lay back, weight on her hands and knees slightly spread to expose the juncture of her thighs. She revealed her glossy pink sex, divulging the strength of her need. So flushed. So wet.

Reese placed his hands on her knees and slid his palms over her skin, sliding up her thighs until he reached her hips. Then he retreated, retracing his path and sensitizing her skin to his touch. When he reached the curve of her hip once more, he traced the intimate crease where her thigh met her pussy. Slow and easy, gentle and sweet, he taunted his mate.

Jane rocked her hips, shifting from side to side, probably attempting to direct his movements. Didn't she realize she was mating an alpha? He always got his way. Always. And right now, his way was a series of tormenting caresses.

He reached with his thumb and traced her pink slit, gathering a hint of the moisture coating her sex. Up and down, collecting a little more with each pass until he couldn't wait any longer. He brought his thumb to his lips, digit glistening with her cream. Eyes on Jane, he slipped it between his lips and the salty tang of her musk danced over his taste buds.

He released his thumb with a pop followed by a rumbling growl. "Delicious."

"You're going to drive me crazy."

Reese smirked. "You love it."

Jane nibbled her lower lip and slowly nodded, her eyes dark with need and face flushed from passion.

"You'll love this, too." He reached for that pink pussy again, hand returning to her thigh. But instead of teasing her, he went for the little bundle of nerves that would make her scream. He slipped through the seam of her lower lips, her juices easing the way for his intimate caress. He sought her clit, easily finding the nub in her folds.

"*Reese*," she hissed and threw back her head, back arched as she rocked against his thumb.

He grinned and watched her face, moving his thumb in small circles and observing her every reaction. He loved it when she whined. Loved the soft whimpers and the deep groans that came from stroking her clit. Jane spread her thighs even further, legs parted in invitation—an invitation he was desperate to accept.

"I'm right here, sweetheart," he murmured and eased closer, lowering until his mouth was even with her core. "And things are only going to get better."

"More?" she rasped.

"Everything. You want my tongue on this sweet pussy? Want me to taste you?" He didn't wait for his mate to answer. He simply withdrew his thumb and brought his mouth to the apex of her sex.

He lapped at her center, gathering the musky dew of her need on his tongue as he moved.

"Yes." She whined. "I want that."

"Anything you want is yours. Anything." His voice came out gritty and raw. Strained because he battled to keep the wolf at bay.

Reese circled her clit with his tongue, tapping the bundle of nerves with rapid flicks before continuing his exploration. He traveled south, teased her center and gathered more of her intimate sweetness. Her core tightened around his tongue as her body seemed to beg to be filled. He was anxious to give her everything she craved. When he was ready.

He gave her a long, leisurely lick along her slit, exploring her silken folds. It'd been five months since he'd reveled in her passion. It was like learning her body anew.

Up and down he traveled, nibbling and licking her, flicking his tongue and making her scream. Then he soothed her with slow laps of her clit. He repeated the caresses, memorizing her scent and taste.

He massaged her thighs, touching every part of her he could reach. He hadn't remembered how soft and sleek she was. Hadn't recalled how she trembled beneath his palms.

"Reese…" There was a plea hidden in her voice.

"What do you want, baby? Tell me."

"Need," she whimpered.

"Need what?" he murmured against her pussy lips. "My mouth?" He ran the flat of his tongue across her clit. "Or something else?"

Jane whined and gripped the cushions, squeezing them tightly. "Claim me. Make me yours. No more teasing."

"I wanted to taste you. Make you come on my tongue before you come on my cock."

"*Please*," she whimpered. "Need you to claim me. Need to feel you inside me. Been so long."

Too long as far as Reese was concerned. His wolf

agreed, the beast nudging him to take Jane for their own.

"Fuck it," he murmured and eased back to sit on his heels. He rolled to his feet and tugged on the button of his jeans. Another pull had his zipper lowering until his cock sprung free of the fabric confines.

And Jane watched it all. Those passion-glazed eyes remained locked on him, tracing his every movement. He shoved at his jeans until they fell from his hips, dropping into a heap at his feet. He kicked them aside, not caring where they fell. He only had eyes for Jane.

Jane with her plump breasts, silken skin and delicious pussy.

"You're the sexiest woman alive."

She skirted his gaze, cheeks turning pink while she avoided his stare.

Reese leaned over her, one finger beneath her chin encouraging her to look at him. She finally met his stare, uneasiness in those eyes. "I mean it. You're beautiful—perfect."

"Fat."

"Pregnant," he countered. "With my pup."

He reached for her hands, skating his fingers down her arms until he reached hers. He twined their digits together and gave her a gentle tug until she stood. He drew her away from the seat, pulling her toward the bed she'd occupied overnight. He didn't waste any time once he reached their destination, quickly encouraging her to spread out across the narrow bed.

Jane was bare before him, body just as perfect as he remembered. More so now that she sheltered his child within her body.

"Reese?" She held out a hand, reaching for him. "Come to me."

Tonight would be an auspicious one—the night he claimed his mate—and it took all his self-control not to pounce on her now.

With a deep breath, he clenched his fists and eased onto the bed, settling on his knees between her spread thighs. He didn't think he'd ever get enough of this view, his mate exposed for him—wanting and waiting for him. Her chest rose and fell with her heavy panting breaths and her dusky nipples were hard, pointed tips. When he let his gaze travel south, he spied the part of her he could only describe as "heaven."

Her pussy was sleek and wet for him.

No woman in his past had ever made him feel this way—like he was the luckiest wolf in the world simply because he got to gaze at her naked body.

"What are you staring at?" Her cheeks flushed a pretty rose.

"You." He grinned. "Just looking at you and thanking God you're mine."

Her lips softened to form a gentle smile. "You're not so bad yourself. I can hardly believe..."

You're mine. He could practically hear the words even though she didn't say them aloud.

"Me neither." In spite of everything pulling them apart, this felt perfect. Like fate took everything in hand and pushed them together despite their problems.

The mattress creaked beneath them as he changed position, tugging her closer while he took a moment to study her body. She shivered and he had no idea if it was in anticipation or if the night's chill had somehow invaded the cabin. Goosebumps raised on her skin and he stroked her arms, palms sliding across her soft skin and brushing them away. Then he followed the path of his hands, kissing every inch of her body until he reached her mouth.

Reese dropped a soft kiss to her lips, only retreating slightly. "Are you ready?" She gave him a shaky nod and he smiled down at her, awed by her trust. It wasn't an easy thing for a wolf to bare their neck and invite a bite, but that's what Jane would soon do for him. "Good."

He trailed kisses down her neck, pausing to flick the shell of her ear. He licked and loved her skin until she released a soft moan and shifted against him, hips wiggling.

"Tell me what you want," he reminded her.

"This. You. This is what I want." Her soft voice filled the quiet room.

He kissed lower still, mouth brushing the swell of her breasts as he cupped her hips. He rolled against her, his thick cock sliding along her wet slit. The hot caress both sated and inflamed his need. So much yet not enough at the same time.

He soon found her nipple, the firm nub seeming to beg for his mouth. He rolled his tongue over the stiff nub and then drew it into his mouth, sucking deep. He laved the sensitive bit of flesh, teasing and tormenting her. She sank her hands into his hair, fisting the strands and tugging as if she could direct his movements. He was all alpha. He'd make love to her as *he* wished. She could get her way next time.

Jane arched into him and he tightened his grip on her hips, grinding against her soaked pussy. Her hot, slick channel beckoned him, promising him hour after hour of pleasure. A pleasure he'd been longing for since their one explosive night together. He nudged her clit with the head of his cock, teasing her with what was to come. She whimpered and whined, whispering words and begging for him to take her.

Take and fill and claim.

He should tease her more, prolong the moment until neither of them could stand the delay another second, but he couldn't help himself. Not when the promise of perfection lingered so near. He lifted his head, releasing her nipple with an audible pop. Jane released his hair and scraped her long nails down his arms, the sharp points scratching his human skin.

Reese reached between them, the heat of her pussy bathing his hand in warmth while he gripped the base of his cock. He adjusted his hips enough to place the tip of his dick at her entrance, her core kissing the end of his shaft. He eased into her, a shallow penetration that tormented them both as he gave her short thrusts. Just enough to give them hints of what could be. He delayed their mutual pleasure, drawing it out even more.

"*Reese*. Please, please, please..." She lifted one leg and hooked it around his waist, muscles flexing as if she could force him to fill her.

"Shhh... I'll give you what you need."

Jane whimpered and wiggled her hips when he next dipped into her core. Fuck but that nearly sent him hurtling over the edge. Then she clenched around him, a tightening of her sheath that broke what little control remained.

Reese leaned over her, their gazes locked, and slowly fed her pussy his cock, inch by agonizing inch. Her silken wetness embraced him in a wet, velvet glove, massaging his shaft as he gave her more and more. She rippled around him once again, squeezing his hard length.

When their hips finally met, bodies melded as intimately as possible, his wolf howled with relief and hunger. Pleasure consumed him, both halves of him overjoyed at connecting with his mate once again. She felt even better than he remembered and it took all of his restraint not to bite her at that moment.

"Reese," she gasped and reached for him. She cupped his cheeks and he let her pull him down, meeting her mouth in a passionate kiss. Their tongues tangled in a sensual imitation of what was to come.

There would be no holding back now. Not anymore. He wanted her to feel everything, every hint of his need for her. His tongue swept out to greet hers and her channel milked his length, urging him to move.

Which he did. Gladly.

Reese settled into a tormenting pace—one that taunted them both. He thrust in and then slowly withdrew, drawing out her moans and groans with every flex of muscle. Their hips met in a carnal rhythm that drove his need higher and higher. His balls slapped against her ass while his pubic bone rubbed her clit. He angled his hips slightly, searching for the spot that would make his mate scream and...

And he found her G-spot, the head of his cock stroking the bundle of nerves as he fucked her. Jane clawed at him, nails digging into his skin, and his wolf howled with joy. So hot. So perfect.

Jane rippled around him, the constant squeeze and release milking his cock and drawing his orgasm closer. In and out he drove into her and she panted along with him, her gaze never straying from his face.

"Claim me," she breathed, her wolf's amber eyes locked on his.

Reese felt his own wolf taking control, eyesight flickering to his beast's while his fangs pushed through his gums. "Yesss..."

He picked up his pace, their bodies meeting in an ever-increasing rhythm while he fought to bring her to her peak. He pushed deep inside her, reveling in the delicious ripple of her inner walls. She was close, so fucking close, and that perfect moment would be here soon.

He turned his head and laved her skin, lapping at the juncture of her neck and shoulder. His release drew closer, anticipation and excitement shoving him toward the precipice. He scraped her damp skin with his fangs, imitating what would soon come, and then he felt it—Jane was breaking apart. She rolled her hips and met him thrust for thrust, commanding her pleasure. His balls drew up as she stiffened and constricted around him, squeezing nearly to the point of pain.

Without hesitation, he struck hard and fast, sinking

his teeth into her flesh in a single, blurred motion. His teeth pierced skin and muscle just as Jane released her final cry of ecstasy. She trembled and jerked beneath him, nails digging deep into his back.

Jane's blood filled his mouth, the coppery fluid coating his tongue, sliding over his taste buds and then slipping down his throat. His wolf howled in approval, relishing the new connection, the physical and mental ties that now bound him and Jane. He took another swallow, one more before he forced his jaws to open and release her wounded shoulder.

He pulled back and fucked her hard in quick, greedy thrusts. The bed shook and banged against the wall while he took what pleasure he could from her lush body until... Until his own release jolted through him, overtaking every other thought and feeling in his body. Pulse after pulse of bliss flooded his system while his cock throbbed within Jane's wet sheath. His cum spurted from the end of his cock, filling her with his seed and branding her with his scent.

They were tied now, physically and mentally. Their scents entwined just as their minds were now bound.

He trembled and twitched, the last vestiges of pleasure slowing while the rapid beat of his heart eased and sluggish calm invaded. He slumped forward, and then carefully eased to her side, pulling her against him as he got comfortable.

Jane curled into him with a soft sigh, body relaxed and boneless.

Reese pressed a kiss to her forehead. "Did I hurt you?"

She shook her head and gave him a pleasure-tinged moan. "It was incredible. Better than anything I've ever felt."

"Not true." He grinned. "We've had sex before."

She shook her head. "Not like this. The claiming... the connection. I feel you," she pressed a hand to her heart. "Here. It's..."

"Perfection."

JANE'S SOFT RHYTHMIC BREATHING HAD ALMOST lulled Reese to sleep when an unfamiliar noise filtered through his slumber. Leaves crunching, murmuring voices, shuffling footsteps. He'd almost decided it was just the wind rustling through the trees when a loud voice boomed through the cabin.

"Where's my daughter, you son of a bitch!"

Reese bolted to his feet in less than a heartbeat. Jane was still rubbing the sleep from her eyes as he yanked on his jeans and then sprinted for the door. Outside, Lance Coleman stood alone at the bottom of the wooden steps, legs spread and his fists propped on his hips. The man's pungent scent nearly knocked Reese over—sweet and sickly at the same time with a hint of rot. Something was definitely wrong with him, but Reese couldn't pinpoint the illness. He'd never smelled anything quite like it before.

"Daddy!"

Jane moved to brush past Reese, but he blocked her path. Her father didn't look as if he was in the mood for a heartwarming family reunion. In fact, the flash of hate in his eyes when Jane came into view reinforced Reese's decision to hold her back.

"You *whore*! How *dare* you leave Coleman lands to cavort with Warren scum!"

Behind Reese, Jane gasped and clutched at his arm. Fear, worry, and pain wafted off her in waves, and his wolf struggled to be set free. It wanted to avenge his mate. Now. Remembering his promise to save her parents, Reese took a deep breath to calm himself, but the elder Coleman wasn't making it easy.

"And you!" the crazed alpha screamed, shifting his attention to Reese. "Do Warrens have such little respect for family that they would come between a father and his daughter?"

Reese fisted his hands, but Jane's presence kept him grounded. "Would you come between an alpha and his mate?"

Lance stumbled backward, as if Reese had struck him. "Your...*what*?"

"My mate," Reese replied quietly, hoping a soft, soothing tone would cool the man's rage.

It didn't.

Lance's wild gaze finally fell on the fresh mark on Jane's neck and his face turned an alarming shade of deep red. He sputtered for a moment before taking two aggressive steps forward.

Reese pushed her behind him and snarled loudly. "You hit her once in my presence, but you will never hurt her again. Do you understand? She no longer belongs to your pack. She's a Warren."

Lance faltered and confusion, or maybe it was regret, filled his haggard face. "I never meant to..."

Another figure stepped out from behind a tree. The Coleman beta—Jane had called him Ian—leaned toward his alpha, a conniving gleam evident in his eye, even at a distance.

"I can't believe she betrayed you like that, sir," he murmured softly, but it was loud enough for Reese to hear it.

"I can't believe you betrayed me like that, Jane!" Lance echoed.

Jane cowered behind Reese. His blood boiled that the little weasel seemed to have so much power over her father. That stopped tonight, one way or another.

"A true alpha would challenge him. Don't you think?" Ian continued.

Lance rolled his shoulders back, and after a moment's pause, shouted. "I challenge you to a fight to the death!"

"No!" Jane cried, once again lurching to put herself between Reese and her father.

Reese spun around and grabbed her shoulders, forcing her to meet his eyes. "Do you trust me?" he whispered.

Her terrified gaze flicked between him and her father before settling on him fully. Reese felt the bond between them tighten and then a reassuring calm smoothed the worry lines on Jane's brow.

"I do," she whispered.

The last thing Reese wanted to do was kill Lance Coleman. That shithead Ian, maybe, but not Lance. He was clearly ill, and killing him would bring no honor to the Warren pack. But Reese was the alpha of his pack, and the alpha of their enemy had just challenged him. He had no choice but to accept. Turning back to Lance, he took one step forward, his lips pressed into a grim line.

"I accept."

Ian's face lit up, but Lance simply turned and walked toward the middle of the clearing. Jane's trembling fingers wiggled into his hand and he squeezed tightly as he led her down the steps. He stopped at a safe distance and asked again, "Do you trust me?"

She nodded, tears slipping down her cheeks. He longed to wipe them away, but he couldn't quite yet. He had to fight her father first.

Fuck.

As he approached Lance, a movement caught his eye. Someone else was hiding behind a tree. How many Coleman men had Lance brought along?

"Show yourself!" Reese shouted.

He nearly lost his breath when he saw who stepped from the shadows, clearly in support of the Coleman alpha. Declan, the young sentry who'd questioned him about Jane.

"You!" he growled. "You betray your alpha this way?"

Declan snorted. "You're no alpha. If you were, just looking at that bitch would make you sick."

If Lance hadn't been there waiting to rip his throat out, Reese would have done the same to Declan. The traitor must have sensed Reese's idea because he turned and bolted into the woods. As desperately as he wanted to chase down Declan and do things that would make the traitor beg for death, it would have to wait.

Reese turned his attention to Lance, who was practically frothing at the mouth. With a heavy sigh, Reese nodded.

"Let's do this."

CHAPTER 10

"Daddy, please," Jane pleaded, keeping a safe distance from him and the man who'd somehow turned her own father against her. "Don't do this."

Lance Coleman's gaze didn't even flick in her direction—something she should have been used to by now, though it cut her deeply anyway. He simply turned to Reese, his wolf so close to the surface, a fine dusting of golden hair sprouted all over his body.

"Look at you," he sneered at Reese. "You thought you were such hot shit after your father died. Thought you could do whatever you wanted. Thought you could kill my beta and get away with it!"

A vein in Reese's neck pulsed with anger, but his outside appearance remained calm. "For the last time, I didn't kill—"

Lance rolled right over him with a derisive snort. "You can't even get your own pack to remain loyal. What's that say about you?"

Reese opened his mouth to answer, but Lance cut him off again.

"I'd say it's because they don't trust their new hot shit alpha." His gaze moved from Reese to Jane, and the pure hate he leveled on her nearly made her retch. "After all, who'd follow an alpha that fucks an enemy bitch?"

Jane had suffered through her father's disappointment in her before, but she'd always known in her heart that his lectures and rebukes came from a place of love. No matter their differences, regardless of how often they argued, she'd always felt secure that their bond would never break. But the moment his cold, crazed eyes landed on her, she realized the man standing before her mate was no longer her father. Somehow, he'd morphed into a shell that was now filled with hate and avarice. If any doubt remained, his next words clenched it.

"And when this piece of shit upstart is lying in the dirt, the veins from his neck still lodged in my teeth, you'll be next. You and that demon spawn in your belly. I swear it."

Shock and grief knocked Jane off balance, and she stumbled backward, though no distance was far enough away to erase the memory of his threat. Even her wolf, who wouldn't hesitate for a second to defend the pup growing inside her, whimpered. A sob choked her for a moment and tears spilled freely down her face.

Then warmth swirled around her, embracing her, soothing her. Reese. Their mate bond meant they could sense each other's emotions, even communicate silently. It only took a single beat of her heart before she calmed. Then she sent him a message only he could hear.

The time has come to end this. Defend yourself, no matter the outcome. My allegiance is to you, my mate, my love, my alpha.

She hoped Reese would be able to diffuse the situation peacefully, but if not, she didn't want him to hesitate for her sake. Without taking his eyes off Lance, he gave her a small nod. He understood.

"Lance, it's not too late to stop this," he growled,

stepping forward. His shoulders were braced and his head was held high, like the alpha he was. "But I won't allow you to threaten my mate and our baby...*your* grandchild."

Jane's father blinked and glanced her way. For a moment, she thought she saw a flicker of...*something* other than hate in them. Then Ian whispered in his ear. Lance's attention snapped back to Reese, burning as hot as ever.

"That abomination is nothing to me. She chose her side when she mated with you, and now she'll suffer the consequences of betraying me."

Reese restrained himself, and Jane sensed how difficult it was for him to control his instincts. Their brief window to bring this to a peaceful conclusion was closing fast.

"Lance, stop listening to that sniveling, conniving runt," Reese said through gritted teeth. "You're not right in the head, my friend."

Ian glared at Reese and then shot a glance over his shoulder toward the tree line. Jane scanned the area, but saw nothing. Still a heavy sense of unease —*more* unease—set her nerves jangling. But her father saw none of it. He simply barked out a harsh laugh.

"Friend! That's a joke. Don't pretend you give two shits about me, my pack or my family!"

"But I do, Daddy," Jane said quietly. "You need to see a healer. All of this—" She waved her hands around them. "—it's not you."

Nostrils flaring, Lance turned to his daughter. "How would you know? You abandoned us, not once but twice! If anyone's changed, it's you. I can't even look at you. I'm ashamed my daughter is such a wh—"

Before anyone could register the movement, Reese lunged at Lance and slapped him across the face. Hard. The sound of skin meeting skin rang through the small clearing, followed by Lance's sharp grunt of pain and surprise.

The grunt turned into a growl of outrage as Lance released his sandy-haired wolf. Jane had always marveled at her father's speed in shifting, but before all four paws hit the dirt, Reese's black wolf waited, ready for a fight. The fur running down his spine lifted in warning, as if his dripping fangs weren't enough of one.

The two alphas circled each other like a vicious yin and yang—one light, one dark. Only once they started moving did Jane notice how frail her father's wolf had grown. Unless her mind was playing tricks on her, his shoulders and hindquarters—once beefy and bulging—appeared shrunken and stringy. Her breaking heart sank into the pit of her stomach and beat double-time as she waited for one to make the first move.

Ian stood across from her, his face glowing with zeal. The bloodlust gleaming in his eyes turned to impatience after the alphas continued circling rather than fighting. He flicked his hand toward the tree line and then six of her father's biggest enforcers emerged from the dense vegetation. They crept up on the pacing wolves until Ian flashed another hand signal, and they stopped in their tracks, their keen eyes never moving from their leader.

Of course!

Ian had never planned on waiting for the outcome of the fight because he knew what it would be. Reese would prevail, presumably by tearing Jane's ill father to shreds. At that point, Ian and his goons—most likely *just* the goons—would jump into the fray and murder Reese.

Ian would no doubt claim they were justified because Reese killed their alpha, but Jane understood the truth immediately. Somehow, in a way she couldn't yet comprehend, Ian had orchestrated this entire thing so he could seize control of the Coleman pack.

Before she could warn Reese, Ian hissed at Lance. "Do it! Now!"

That was all her father's wolf needed to lunge for Reese's throat. Reese deftly avoided the gnashing fangs, leaping sideways and spinning around to brace himself for another attack. Lance stumbled at the near-miss, but quickly regained his feet and planted himself in an aggressive stance.

Reese remained motionless, waiting. He waited for her. He could take out her father in a single swipe of his massive paw, yet he didn't. He held himself—and his wolf—in check, hoping for some resolution other than death. She couldn't have picked a better mate if she'd tried.

Lance darted forward, much faster than before, and managed to catch a mouthful of fur along Reese's neck. Jane screamed at the same moment Reese shook off the other wolf. Again, Reese held firm, allowing Lance to bring himself to his feet. But instead of looking at his opponent, her father's feral gaze fell on Jane. His teeth pulled back in a sinister snarl, and before she could blink, he leapt at her.

This proved to be Reese's breaking point. Without

hesitation, he tackled the older wolf. They rolled in the dirt, jaws snapping, until Reese came out on top, a single paw planted squarely on Lance's throat. Saliva from Reese's exposed fangs dripped down on Lance's fur.

This was it. The end. Reese's superior strength had subdued Lance. His only choice was to submit to the superior alpha. Relief brought tears to Jane's eyes. Her father would live, and they would force him to get the help he needed.

Apparently, Ian realized the same thing, but he wasn't nearly as happy as Jane. A heavy sweat broke out on his brow and he looked back at his goons. They seemed just as unsure of themselves, which only seemed to fuel Ian's worry.

"Fight, you idiot!" he shouted frantically at Lance. "Roll! Do *something!*"

Reese glanced back at Ian, most likely to make sure the sneaky bastard wasn't trying to sneak up on him. It was just the distraction Lance needed to reach up and chomp down on Reese's ear.

Howling in surprise, Reese faltered, which allowed Lance to knock him off-balance. Jane's mate flailed backward as her father scrambled to stay on top of him. Reese fended off Lance's gnashing teeth until they sank deep into his forearm.

"No!" Jane screeched. As much as she wanted her father to live, she wasn't about to stand by and watch him kill her mate. If she died in the process...well, at least she'd go down fighting rather than waiting to be torn apart by her father or Ian.

Calling her wolf forward, she'd just started her shift when Reese managed to get his hind feet under Lance and kick him off. Darting forward, he clamped onto Lance's exposed throat and pinned him down.

Now a different voice screamed, "No!" Ian rushed toward the wolves, but he was knocked to the ground by a blur of white and red. Jane had to blink three times before she believed what her eyes told her. Ginger Coleman kneeled before Reese, hands clasped together, pleading with him.

"Please allow him to live," she begged. "Please!"

The world went still as everyone waited for his decision. As the victor, it was his choice whether to dole out vengeance or mercy. He chose mercy. Lance crumpled into Ginger's waiting arms, and she held his battered and bleeding head in her lap.

"Shh," she cooed as she stroked his fur.

Ian exploded in rage. "No! Attack him, you pathetic old man! Kill!!"

Lance raised his head, trying to locate Reese. A growl rumbled out of him as he set his sights and then tried to get back on his feet, but Ginger held his weak body tightly.

"Lance, I'm here now." Her voice was consoling, but firm. "Listen to my voice. I know you're in there, Lance. Please come back to me."

Lance growled again, but no longer tried to pull away from her. The fire in his eyes flickered, but didn't go out completely. Ginger glanced over her shoulder at her daughter, and Jane gasped when she saw the vibrant purple bruise on her mother's cheek. Her father had been erratic and cruel lately, but never in a million years would he willingly hurt his mate. It wasn't in their nature as werewolves. Mates *protected* each other against all enemies and against all odds.

"Lance," her mother continued, "do you remember the day Jane was born? It was the happiest day of your life. Remember that? Remember the way she squalled? Remember how her tiny little fingers wrapped around your thumb for the first time?"

"Shut up, you bitch!" Ian screamed. "You're ruining everything!"

When he moved toward the couple, Reese put himself between Ian and Jane's parents. The hackles on his neck raised to their full height and his deep, warning snarl sent shivers up *her* spine. Wimpy Ian must have wet himself! Even the Coleman enforcers backed away from the massive alpha protecting his family—as sick and twisted as they may have been.

"Lance, my love, my very life, hear my voice and come back to me. You're sick and you need to see a healer. We can fix this. We can cure you, but you need to stop listening to others and listen to me."

Lance's growls grew quieter, but he never stopped, and his eyes remained locked on Reese. Ginger had finally had enough.

"Lance Coleman, stop that right now!"

Everyone in the clearing jumped a little at her sharp command, including Lance, who whimpered in response. Sighing deeply, he laid his weary head in his mate's lap and changed back to his human form.

"Oh Lance," Ginger cried, bending over him and cradling his body.

"I'm sorry," Lance whispered into Ginger's shoulder. "Please...help me."

He reached up to hold her, and together they reconnected on a level Jane had never understood before. Now that she'd found her mate, though, she cried for how painful this chasm must have been for her mother. The crazy urge to laugh and cry at the same time overwhelmed Jane. She was about to go to them, to make her family whole once more, when Ian shouted, "This is bullshit!"

In an instant, he'd shifted into his hideous white wolf, as did his enforcers. They flanked him on either side as they stalked toward Reese. He stood his ground, but Jane sensed his apprehension. There were seven of them and only one of him. He might be strong and powerful, but even he had to know his odds were slim.

Before the brute squad could take two steps, though, the air around them filled with the loud rumble of dozens, maybe hundreds, of growls. Jane spun around, heart pounding, to find what looked like the entire Warren pack slinking out of the forest, a legion of brown fur and glistening fangs.

Ian stopped, looking between Reese and the army at his back, and then spun around and bolted for the trees. His enforcers looked confused for a moment, but then they followed suit.

The threat against his mate eliminated, Reese shifted back and gathered Jane into his arms. Burying his nose in her hair, he simply held her, and she breathed him in, happier than she could ever remember.

The insanity was finally over. Ian was gone, her baby was safe, her father would get the help he so desperately needed, and she was tucked up against the bare chest of her mate, her rock, her home.

And no one could ever take that away.

EPILOGUE

*J*ane lowered her quickly expanding body to the first step of their little cabin in the woods. Soon she'd barely be able to sit on a sofa, and she couldn't wait. A smile played on her lips and she absentmindedly rubbed her tummy as she watched the goings-on in the clearing. Or rather, the *not*-goings-on.

The Coleman pack had jammed themselves as close to the tree line as they could on one side, while the Warrens huddled and whispered amongst themselves on the other.

Seventh-graders at their first school dance couldn't look more uncomfortable.

It was to be expected, of course, but she'd had some fantasy that her mating the Warren alpha would magically inspire her people to be happy about merging packs. Reese's people had taken the news well, but the Coleman wolves still weren't sure this entire situation wasn't some kind of elaborate trap to kill them all.

Immediately following the fight between Reese and her father a few weeks earlier, Lance had ceded control of the Coleman pack and all its land to Reese. Then Ginger had spirited him away to the National Healing Center in Ft. Lauderdale. Only after Ian's six enforcers confirmed the story did her old pack believe the events, but that didn't make them happy about the transition. They were Colemans, through and through, and Warrens were their sworn enemies.

A full week after her parents had been at the Healing Center, Jane had finally received news on her father's condition. Lance had been dosed with a slow-acting poison that drove him insane over the course of several months.

The healers had only seen the poison once before, about ten years earlier. The alpha of a pack somewhere in Georgia had created it for his mate to make her more docile and controllable, but his plan backfired when she went feral and killed a human couple. Thankfully, their teenage daughter had survived unscathed, but she'd been forced to watch the rabid wolf tear apart her parents. The National Circle had acted swiftly to put down the insane wolf, and to imprison her mate for not only causing the situation, but for allowing her to run rampant.

Once the healers had been able to identify the poison in Lance's system, treatment was simple. It would take time, but eventually, Lance Coleman would be back to his gruff, demanding, loving ways.

The only question remaining was who'd poisoned him. It didn't take Sherlock Holmes to sniff out the culprit—*Ian*.

As they'd discovered, Ian had been dosing Lance long before Peter had been killed. In fact, they suspected Ian had been planning the murder of his father and Lance for a very long time. With both of them out of the way, he'd believed he would inherit the pack...*and* Jane.

A shudder raised the hairs on Jane's arms at the thought. Then gratitude filled her heart and her eyes with love for her family—old, new, and the one soon to come. She couldn't wait to introduce the little niblet to his or her grandparents, but that would have to wait until Lance was fully healed.

As her gaze swept over the gathering of wolves, Jane realized they were all healing. Ian's treachery had nearly destroyed so many lives. The enforcers he'd recruited had been fed a bunch of lies about Lance going feral. They'd been told that Ian wanted to *save* their alpha from being put down. If his plan had succeeded, the entire Coleman pack might have been banished—not just Ian. She didn't want to think about what would have happened to her and her baby if she hadn't managed to escape. That was behind them now. Today would be the first step toward healing their packs.

The door creaked behind her, and every eye in the clearing turned their focus to the cabin. Her mate's scent hit Jane before she felt his big hand on her back as he crouched beside her. The transition might be rough, but smiling up into Reese's warm eyes, she knew it would all work out.

"Ready?" he whispered.

At her nod, he helped her up. But before addressing the gathered wolves, he leaned down so only she could hear. "Just got off the phone with your father."

Her father had called Reese? *Willingly?* "Is he okay?"

Reese smiled at the implication her father would have to be insane to reach out to his new son-in-law.

"He's fine. Well, better anyway. He wanted to tell me —" Reese paused to clear a frog that had suddenly lodged in his throat. "He wanted to tell me how sorry he was about my dad. He said long ago, farther back than he could remember, they'd been friends. Whatever had caused their falling out—his memory is still fuzzy from the poison—Lance says he regrets not mending fences when he could."

Tears sprang into Jane's eyes, which wasn't completely unexpected. She cried a lot these days, mostly happy tears.

"That's so good to hear," she said, her voice squeaking with emotion.

"I just wanted you to know. Now let's do this—"

Brody jogged up to them before Reese could finish. "Sorry to interrupt, but I thought you'd like to know the sentries have confirmed Ian is off our combined lands. He's no longer a threat."

Reese nodded curtly, his lips pressed together. Exile was no slap on the wrist for their kind. It was a fate worse than death, and the sentence was not handed down lightly. Ian was doomed to wander around alone, with no alpha to ground him and no pack to support him, until he lost his mind and went feral. He'd probably get shot by some human protecting his animals or family from a rabid wolf. It was no less than he deserved, but still difficult to think about.

Jane sent up a small prayer of gratitude that her idiotic plan to live in the human world hadn't worked out. No doubt she would have become just another statistic. She never would have found the eternal bond of her true mate, the support of a pack twice the size of what it might have been, and a pup to raise without fear of being discovered.

Reese clapped his hands, snapping Jane out of her thoughts and drawing the attention of both packs. Blond and brunet heads swiveled toward them, staring at their powerful alpha.

"Today is an important day, maybe the most important in any of our lives," he started, addressing both sides of the clearing. "Today we join together to create a single, unified, powerful pack."

Light murmurs, mostly from the Colemans, drifted across the crowded space. Many still weren't sure this was a good idea, and who could blame them. After all, their packs had been enemies for as long as Jane could remember. But if anyone could unite them, it was Reese.

"Both packs have endured heartache over the last year," he continued. "We lost our alpha, but you Colemans have lost so much more. You probably feel as if you've lost everything—your alpha, your homelands, your very identity as a pack. Which is why I've decided that Colemans will *not* become Warrens."

More murmurs as Colemans glanced at each other, worried about what this new enemy alpha had planned for them. One brave female stepped forward, her voice shaking as she spoke. "So, you're going to exile us as well?"

Reese's face softened, and he smiled at the woman. Jane leaned in and whispered, "That's Claudia."

"No, Claudia," he said without missing a beat, "you're a member of my pack now, and I will fight to protect you, even if that means my own death. But too much pain exists between the Colemans and the Warrens, so we will be known as neither. From this day forward, we are the Wilde Ridge pack!"

CELIA KYLE & MARINA MADDIX

A brief moment of shocked silence fell over the crowd. Then the world exploded with whoops, hollers and cheers. Colemans and Warrens—no, *ex*-Colemans and *ex*-Warrens—crossed the space between them and started shaking hands, some even hugged, however briefly. Thankfully, no one was in their wolf form, or there most certainly would have been a fair amount of butt sniffing going on.

Once the commotion died down a little, Brody dropped to his knee before Reese and then whipped out a huge hunting knife and pressed the edge to the back of his forearm. "I would be honored to become the first to pledge my fealty to the Wilde Ridge pack. I freely offer my own blood as my sacred oath of allegiance to you, my alpha."

Before Brody could cut himself, Reese stopped him. "I must do one thing first, before I receive anyone else."

It was Reese's turn to drop to his knees... right in front of Jane. She looked around her, thoroughly confused. Then he took her hands in his and placed them on her tummy.

"Jane, I vow to you all of my loyalty and love until the end of time. For you, I would move heaven and earth. Will you join me in leading our new pack to a happy and prosperous future?"

Once again, the tears flowed, but Jane knew her hormones had nothing to do with it this time. This time it was all about love. She gazed over the newly united pack and was met by smiles and even more tears. Until her dying day, she would never forget this moment.

Nodding, tears dripping all over Reese's upturned face, she shouted her answer. "Yes!"

The pack broke out into more applause and cheers while Reese leaned into to drop a kiss on her stomach. Just then, the baby kicked, and kicked *hard*, right against Reese's lips.

Jane sniffed back her tears and laughed. "I think the baby agrees too."

IF YOU ENJOYED THIS BOOK, PLEASE BE TOTALLY awesomesauce and leave a review so others may discover it as well. Long review or short, your opinion will help other readers make future purchasing decisions. So, go forth and rate our level-o-awesome!

Interested in more Howls Romances from Celia Kyle & Marina Maddix?

The Alpha Shifter's Family Reunion - He will protect his mate from all threats. Even her own father!

Her Desert Panther Princes - Mating isn't in their plans, but plans can shift as fast as the panther princes of Adikar.

ABOUT THE AUTHORS

CELIA KYLE

Ex-dance teacher, former accountant and erstwhile collectible doll salesperson, New York Times and USA Today bestselling author Celia Kyle now writes paranormal romances. It goes without saying that there's always a happily-ever-after for her characters, even if there are a few road bumps along the way. Today she lives in central Florida and writes full-time with the support of her loving husband and two finicky cats.

Website

Facebook

~

MARINA MADDIX

New York Times & USA Today Bestselling Author Marina Maddix is a romantic at heart, but hates closing the bedroom door on her readers. Her stories are sweet, with just enough spice to make your mother blush. She lives with her husband and cat near the Pacific Ocean, and loves to hear from her fans.

Website

Facebook

Created with Vellum

Made in the USA
Lexington, KY
17 February 2018